An Appetite for Miracles

An Appetite for Miracles

LAEKAN ZEA KEMP

LITTLE, BROWN AND COMPANY
New York Boston

Little, Brown and Company
Hachette Book Group
1290 Avenue of the Americas, New York, NY 10104
Visit us at LBYR.com

First Edition: April 2023

Little, Brown and Company is a division of Hachette Book Group, Inc. The Little, Brown name and logo are trademarks of Hachette Book Group, Inc.

The publisher is not responsible for websites (or their content) that are not owned by the publisher.

Little, Brown and Company books may be purchased in bulk for business, educational, or promotional use. For information, please contact your local bookseller or the Hachette Book Group Special Markets Department at special.markets@hbgusa.com.

Library of Congress Cataloging-in-Publication Data

Names: Kemp, Laekan Zea, author.
Title: An appetite for miracles / Laekan Zea Kemp.
Description: First edition. | New York ; Boston : Little, Brown and Company, 2023. | Audience: Ages 14 & up. | Summary: With the help of her cousin and their friends, Danna scours the city, searching for her grandfather's favorite foods and hoping the remembered flavors will bring back his memories.
Identifiers: LCCN 2022016377 | ISBN 9780316461733 (hardcover) | ISBN 9780316461948 (ebook)
Subjects: CYAC: Novels in verse. | Grief—Fiction. | Dementia—Fiction. | Food—Fiction. | Families—Fiction. | Mexican Americans—Fiction. | LCGFT: Novels in verse.
Classification: LCC PZ7.5.K46 Ap 2023 | DDC [Fic]—dc23
LC record available at https://lccn.loc.gov/2022016377

ISBNs: 978-0-316-46173-3 (hardcover), 978-0-316-46194-8 (ebook)

Printed in the United States of America

LSC-C

Printing 1, 2022

For my grandfather Marcelino.

They took your name and so much more. But with every story. I'm taking it back.

Danna

Alphabet Soup

When I was little
you fed me
alphabet soup.

You placed the spoon
in my hand,
showed me how
to swirl the letters,
scoop them up.

D for Danna.
G for Grandpa.

I used my tongue
to mash
the shapes
against the roof of
my mouth
while you
sounded out
each one.

You showed me
how to move
them
like
constellations.

How to stack them.
Line them up.
Jiggling puzzle pieces.

You showed me
how to ignite
their sounds
on the tip of my tongue.

How to roll
them around
between my cheeks;
chew
on them
between my teeth.

In the bottom of that bowl
we wrote
poems.

We told
stories.

And I know
if you could just
close your eyes,
if you could just
feel
those textures
on your
tongue,
if
you could just
taste
those memories...

Salty.
Sour.
Bittersweet.

You *could* remember.

You could remember me.

Shadow Puppets

Mami's making dinner,
which is never
a good sign.

But Papi's working late tonight
and
Mami's trying
to write poems
too.

To arrange the ingredients
just right.
Using my grandmother's
old recipe cards
to start
a fire
in Grandpa's belly;
to light the way
to his heart,
memories like
shadow puppets
on the walls of
his mind.

"Hand me the pomegranate," she says
with one hand raised.

I watch her break
it open and
I remember once
Grandpa
told me that
the apple Eve plucked
from the Tree of
Knowledge
was

probably
actually
a pomegranate.

As Mami sprinkles the seeds
on top of
the walnut sauce,
I pray there is still
knowledge
in them.

I pray.

I peer
over her shoulder
and say, "He doesn't like parsley."

She doesn't look at me.
"You can't have chiles en nogada without parsley.
It needs to look like the Mexican flag."

So he'll remember,
I almost hear
her think.

So that if the ingredients
aren't
stacked
just
right,
maybe
the
colors
will
be
the
thread.

Tying him back to when he was a boy.

"Are you hungry, Dad?"
Mami puts the plate in front of him.

His spine
curves.
A question
mark.

And then I take his hand.
Help him
hold
the fork
like
he helped me
hold
that spoon.

I help him
eat
Mami's poem.

One bite
at
a
time.

Dear God

I know our
relationship
is not
supposed to be
transactional.

But.

You are
the one
who invented
an eye for an eye,
so,
maybe
I can
entice you
with
a good deal.

Grandpa believes in you.
Like, a lot.

He always used to tell me to pray to you when
        I was scared.
He said you were always watching over us
and that all of our blessings come from you.

I'm not so sure about that.

When I won
the class spelling bee
in sixth grade
it was because I studied
for two months straight.
Not divine intervention.

And when I finally
learned to doggy paddle
it was because I practiced
every weekend
for an entire summer
(after Mami threw me into the pool
and told me
to sink
or swim).

Okay,
maybe
it *was* you
who dragged me
back to the surface
that day
when I thought
I was going to drown.

In fact,
I am willing to
commit
this to memory;
to convince
myself
you saved me.

I am willing to believe,

If
you promise
to fix this mess,
to take the broken pieces
and put my grandpa
back together.

For this,
I will give you my soul

and
my cousin Victoria's too.
(I can be very convincing,
I promise.)

I hear
you like souls.
And mine
is pretty
awesome.

Love,
Danna

Raúl

Nemesis

The ceiling fan
has become
my archnemesis.

In the dark,
the gears grind.

Like my teeth.
Like the thoughts
wedging themselves
between
me and sleep.

Mrs. Perez's cat
slides like a fish
past my bedroom window,
spitting at the moon
I can't see.

All I have to do
is get up
and go to the glass.
To lean against it
and peer out.

But I don't want to look.

I don't want to look
at a moon
my mother
isn't allowed to see.
Hasn't seen.

In seven hundred.
And twenty-nine.
Days.

I reach for the stack
of
letters
by
my
bed.

I take one off
the top,
unfolding
the thick paper,
tracing the raised
ink
that has been
raising me.

For two years.

Two years of
"Sweet dreams, Raúl."
"Do your homework, Raúl."
"Be good to your uncle, Raúl."
"I'm sorry, Raúl."
"I miss you, Raúl."

I miss you too, Mom.

Words.
Prayers.

Sometimes pressed.
Sometimes hammered.
Dark and deep
like tattoo ink.

And when I read them,
I don't hear
the rattle of the air conditioning,
or
my uncle snoring in the next room,
or
the whir of the ceiling fan.

I hear my mother's voice,
ignited between my ears
like a dream.

A dream
I'll have to
wake up
from
the second
I fall
asleep.

Because that's when they come
when they *always* come
to take her
away.

Nobody Knows

When someone dies
people know
exactly what to say.

Not the right thing.
Not the true thing.

But what's socially acceptable.

There is a script
we inherit.

Part of the good human handbook.

But when someone goes to prison
there is no script.

Which means a lot of fumbling,
a lot of forcing. the. words. to. come.

People try their best
with things like:
"Your mother was such a sweet woman."

Is.
She is.

"Your mother would be so proud of how you've
handled this."

Is.
She is.

Or they try and
fail miserably
with things like:
"God works in mysterious ways."

or
"Everything happens for a reason."

I smile,
but behind gritted teeth,
I scream
deep down
in the places where
no one else
can hear,

No.

No, it doesn't.

Then I get up
onstage
with the mediocre
praise band
I've been
practicing with
twice a week
for two years
and I strum,
playing simple
chords
that tie up
the truth.

A salve
to my uncle's sermon,
making it go
down
easy.

"Remember," he tells them,
"to give your pain to God.
Nobody knows
your suffering
like Jesus."

Lost

Sunday School
compounds
my suffering
exponentially.

Even though
they bribe us
with bacon and pancakes,
Manny and I
still spend the whole time
hiding in the back,
listening to
The Mars Volta.

Manny is my friend
by default.
He's the only other kid my age in class
and sometimes
he tells jokes that are actually funny.
Other times, he laughs alone.

But he doesn't mind.
I appreciate that.

He also plays the drums
and on days
when it feels like I'm being smushed
by a giant thumb,
I'll show up at his house,
unannounced,
and he'll let me beat back the feeling,
knuckles blanched around the drumsticks,
sweat pouring
down
my
face.

Heart pounding.
Pounding.

And he never asks why;
never asks questions.

He just listens.

Unlike Señora de Souza,
the Sunday school teacher,
who asks so many questions,
too many questions.

That I can't answer.
That no one can.

So we sit
in the uncomfortable
silence, waiting for
the Holy Spirit
to slip down
over our skin,
for Faith
to burrow
like a beetle
into our hearts.

For it to war
with the doubts
inside us
and win.

And for those
who've already lost,
we pretend.

Every day,
we pretend.

So when Señora de Souza asks,
"Raúl, would you like to
lead us
in our closing prayer?"
I smile
and nod
and speak
to a God
I know
isn't listening.

Danna

Sunday Cena

Thank God
Papi is cooking
dinner tonight.

Mami is busy
telling Aunt Veronica
about the drama
at work. "I did
everything and
she took all
the credit."

Uncle Moises
is flipping
channels on
the TV. "I've
got a hundred
on this game."

My cousin Victoria
is scrolling
through social,
waiting for me
to finish helping
Papi with dinner.
"Is it ready yet?"

Grandpa is
sitting
and
watching
the floor.

Like the sounds
of their voices
are cracking
something
open
inside him.

I wait
for memories
to slither out.

"See if he wants some."
Papi hands me
a cup of
coffee
because Grandpa
always used to
bring home
a Styrofoam cup
from Gloria's Cafe
after picking up
the Sunday paper.

Tall,
dark roast,
with a shot
of vanilla.

I blow on it,
steam billowing up
like tiny clouds
like ghosts.

You are not one yet.

I take his fingers,
so cold,
and press them
against

the warm
mug.

He smiles
and it's like
watching an
old photograph
come to life.

"Danna…"

I blink,
not sure if
I just
imagined it.

Mami and Aunt Veronica
choke on their words,
quiet.

Uncle Moises
turns the volume down on the TV,
staring.

Victoria
stops mid-text,
mouth open wide.

Papi
drops
an
egg.
It splatters on the floor.

"You better clean up
that mess
before
your mother
finds it,"
Grandpa says.

Grandpa says,
in a voice
that is a glimpse
from the past,
peeling
himself
from the confines
of that two-dimensional
photograph
that is his disease;
he wakes up.

He *remembers*.

My grandmother.
Aurora.
His North Star.

And as I kneel
in front of him
I pray
that something
of her
still
twinkles in my eyes.

That he will find it
and hold on.

~~That if he remembers~~

That *when* he remembers
that she is dead,
he will hold on.

Fault Lines

In between
bites
we take turns
joking, talking, asking questions.

To keep him
in this time and place.

Even though stillness
is against his nature.

Even though
he was as in love
with going somewhere new
as he was with Aurora.

And as I watch Victoria
pepper him with questions
I realize that's what I miss most.

Going with him.

Every meal
and every story
making me believe
I had been there too.

Like the world belonged
to the both of us.

Like it was ours to devour.

"Weren't you worried it might erupt?"
Victoria leans forward,
listening.

"Lanzarote has been sleeping
since 1824. I was more worried
about the geothermal heat
drying out the chicken."

"Five stars?" Victoria asks.

"Two out of five
for the food."
Grandpa winks.
"Five out of five
for the sunset."

He looks past us,
remembering
a sherbet sky.

"It was like
the mountains
were on fire.
A snapshot
of what those
fault lines
were truly
capable of."
He whistles
between his teeth.

"I wish I could have
taken a bite out of that."

Seconds

I'm so wrapped up
in Grandpa's stories
about getting lost
while truffle hunting
in Florence
and hugging the deck
while snow crab fishing
in Alaska
and eating fermented shark
in Iceland
before waking up
to a midnight sun
that I almost
don't sense
her staring

at my empty plate,

at my hand reaching for
the basket of croquettes.

Victoria sees Mami
and me
in a standoff.
"These are delicious,
Tío," Victoria says,
reaching for more too.

"Here, kiddo"—
Papi tries to spoon
more food onto my plate—
"there's plenty."

Mami raises an eyebrow.

I sink
in my chair.

She waits
for her voice
to needle inside,
shoving away
my own thoughts.

*A second
on the lips
for a
lifetime
on the hips.*

The words lasso me.

I turn to Papi
and say,
"I'm
full."

Just Like You

Across the table
Grandpa winks again.
"Too full for dessert?"

I smile,
remembering
the poem
at the bottom
of the fridge—
the Key lime pie
I made yesterday
because
Grandpa
always said
they taste like

summer rain
and
his mother's hugs
and
fireworks
on the Fourth of July.

If Grandpa had gotten his way
we would have eaten it first,
but Mami's off sugar
and no one gets their way
but her.

Papi brings it to the table
before cutting everyone a slice.

I watch Grandpa closely,
waiting for fireworks.

He takes a big bite.

"It's glorious,"
he says
before looking
at Mami
and then back
at me. "And so are
you."

Lists

If food is the thing that combats
my fears
then lists are the chains
that tie them down.

My grandmother
was always making lists.
Lists for the grocery store. For errands. For Christmas gifts.
For phone calls to the friends who lived just around the cor-
        ner but would rather gossip in separate rooms.
For doctor's appointments, and baby showers, and funerals.

Even for her own.

She had the event planned down to the minute
with a song list, Bible passages, pallbearers, speakers,
        prayers, and flower arrangements.

Everything perfect.

That's how Mami likes things too.
Like her cooking (which is why she doesn't do it very much)
and my body (which is why she is always measuring me
with an invisible scale that seems to change,
to train its eye on new flaws
as soon as
I erase
the old ones).

I make lists
because I know
things are
never perfect.

Because I know
bad things

lurk
around
every corner.

So I make lists
and set traps,
trying
to catch
the bad
before it gets too close.

Trying to write
as many unknowns
as possible
out of my future.

Trying to mold
that future
with my
bare hands.

I grab the notebook on my nightstand
and flip to my latest
trap.

Tikka Masala from Teji's
A Root Beer Float from Big Top's
Pork Dumplings from Wu Chow
Homemade Lasagna
A Bagel and Schmear from Biderman's
Rice Pudding from Casa Costa Bakeshop
Aurora's Mashed Red Beans
Sunny D

A list
of all of the ways
I've tried
to make him
remember.

I write
Coffee
and put a star
next to it,
glad;
relieved
that
the monster
is slain...

at least
for
tonight.

Raúl

Combustible

School
isn't for me.

But it's the only thing
my mom
asks about
on our five-minute
phone calls
once
a week.

Not how I'm doing
or feeling
or drowning
without her.

But whether or not
I'm turning in
my homework on time.
If I'm still getting
As and Bs.
If I finished
that chemistry project
I mentioned.
If my teachers
like me.

I want to tell her,
I don't care.

When Mrs. Choi
hands me back

a failed test,
I want to tell her,
I don't care.

When Mr. Rodriguez
asks me
to stay after school,
I want to scream,
I don't care.

I don't care.
I *don't* care.
I don't.

But then I think about
that five-minute phone call.
Mom's questions.
My answers.

I have to give her answers.

So I take the test
and fix my mistakes.

And I meet Mr. Rodriguez
after school
to practice
balancing chemical equations,
pretending
the elements
are all the things
outside of my control.

My life
in numbers and letters
stacked wrong,
so close to
combustible.

Until Mr. Rodriguez
moves a symbol
here,
a symbol
there,
showing me
how to
make things right.

"You're getting it,"
he says.

And for a split
second,
I wish
I cared.

That I could get it.

That I could make things right.

That it would matter.

Safe

For some reason
Manny chooses
to brave
the cafeteria
every day for lunch.

It is a cesspool,
a lion's den,
the ninth circle of hell.

But he says
they have good
nachos.

I wouldn't know.
I brown-bag it:
a plain cheese quesadilla
burn marks
from where I leave it
too long
on the comal
while I brush my teeth.

After I transferred,
I followed Manny
that first day
to the back of the line,
the smell of
canned cheese
turning
my stomach,
as I looked
out
on a pack of wolves.

But where I saw
snarls and
glinting canines
ready to swallow
me whole,
Manny saw
mouths
primed for laughter;
an expectant audience.

On Sundays,
he's always trying to
steal the show
with drum solos,
and flailing arms.
At school,
he is the show,
telling
the kinds of jokes
only teachers find funny
and then impersonating
those teachers behind their backs
while the other students
laugh hysterically,
phones out
catching
every exaggerated gesture
and quintessential catchphrase.

While he has them
rolling,
I roll out
to a shady spot
in the courtyard
to eat my quesadilla
in peace.

All day
I lug

my guitar
around
on my back,
waiting for the
thirty minutes at lunch
when I can
work out
a new chord
progression,
toy with
a new melody
that's been
stuck
in my head
for days.

The first day,
people pointed;
some laughed.

The next day,
they took
a closer look
at my beat-up
guitar,
face scratched,
and said,
"What happened?
Did you drop it
in the Rio Grande?"

Something the kids
at my old school
never would have said
(instead, they would have
clowned on me
for never even having
been to Mexico;

for mangling the language
como un pocho).

But when they took
my mom,
my school changed too.

Everything changed.

Except
this.

My callused fingers
gripping
the neck of my guitar,
the tinny sounds,
vibrations
waking up
my skin.

Without it,
I'm sleepwalking,
but
inside
those sounds,
I'm safe.

Masks

The flea market
was packed
with tables of ceramics
and bootleg DVDs;
winter coats with the security tags still on them,
old tools and textiles and tajin-covered fruit—

plastic bags full of it
that Mom wouldn't
let me hold
because my hands
were too small.

Even though
all they wanted to do
was touch things.

The soft cobijas
that I pretended
were real tiger fur.

The pocketknives
in leather holders
with Bible verses
embossed on the side.

The squishy conchas
stacked high in clear plastic bags.

My mother's hand.

I circled her
like a fly
and when she swatted
me away
I disappeared down

the aisles,
each row like
the entrance to its own
little world.

Worlds where I could be
Wolverine running from the Texas Rangers
or Zorro avenging my wife's murder
or a gun-slinging outlaw robbing a bank.

Masks I tried on
over and over and over again
until Señor Velasco
snatched me up by the shirt
for running inside
and I looked behind him
and saw a giant wall
of tiny guitars.

Perfect
for my small hands.

And it was like they knew,
reaching before I could
even ask permission.

It was like they *knew*
we'd fit.

Señor Velasco noticed it too,
handing me the instrument.
He adjusted my fingers,
showing me how
to hold down the strings.
How to make them sing
with a single strum.

When Mom finally found me
she was screaming and crying and thanking God
that I was safe.

As she dragged me
through the parking lot
and back to the car
I screamed and cried
just as loud.

And I didn't stop.

I cried all the way home.

I cried in between bites of Hamburger Helper.

I cried in the bath while Mom tried to keep the sham-
poo out of my eyes.

I cried through bedtime prayers
before screaming into my pillow
after she'd closed the door.

I cried
for the world
I finally belonged in;
for the mask
that finally fit.

The One

The next day
Mom was late
and I sat on the steps
with my first grade
teacher Ms. Pham
while the parking
lot emptied
and the sun started
to sink behind
the clouds.

When she finally
pulled up
her makeup was smudged,
her eyes dark.

She kissed me
without a word
and that's when
I noticed the bruise,
purple
and
angry
like something painted on.

Another mask.

Except when she tried to smile
and it didn't quite reach
her eyes. When she winced
I knew
it was real.

We drove in silence
until the car slowed
in the flea market parking lot.

Just as the stall owners
were closing their doors.

We ran,
Mom holding my hand
the whole way
until we reached
Señor Velasco's stall.

He looked up,
surprised to see us.

Then Mom finally spoke.
"Which one, mijo?"

She dug in her purse
for her wallet,
pulling out
a clump of wadded bills.

Señor Velasco
looked down at me.
Then he looked at Mom.

He closed her hand,
pushing the money away,
before reaching
for one of the little guitars,
and saying, "I know just the one."

Armor

Mr. Rodriguez
is waiting for me
after school.

"Glad you could
make it." He smiles
and I almost
let it disarm me.

But then I remember
where I am,
tugging
my armor
tight.

"Thanks for helping me,"
I say, because I know
what adults want to hear.

I hand over my homework
and he starts to scribble,
his red pen
crisscrossing
until the whole thing
is drenched.

A massacre of mistakes.

He looks up at me,
searching.

He sighs. "We've gone
over these, Raúl.
You've been coming in
for tutorials
for weeks. A few days ago

you were really
making progress."

I shrug, not meeting his eyes.

"Is something else going on?"
he asks,
the words
like an arrow
aimed straight
for the only
chink in my armor.

Something, I think.

More like
everything.
And nothing.
My head
both
empty and
bursting at the seams.

"I just don't get it,"
I say,
because it's true.

"You know," he says,
his voice changing,
shrinking,
"when I was your age
my father went to prison.
Armed robbery.
He was locked up
for ten years."
He kneads his hands,
like the memories
still make him
cold.

"Missed
my high school graduation
and my college graduation
and the birth of my first son."

"I'm sorry," I say.

"I'm not telling you
for your sympathy, Raúl.
I'm telling you
because I know.
I know how hard it is
to focus on school,
to think about anything
else."

I just nod.

"But all of this is temporary."
He turns my homework
facedown on his desk.
"And one day
your mother
is going to come home."
He pauses,
waiting for me
to meet his eyes.
"Who will you be
when that happens?"

Danna

Third Period

Six months ago,
when the clock ticked
to 12:50
my heart would leap
into
my
throat.

Because I knew
Yeong Kim,
captain
of the basketball team,
DECA president,
and the only boy
I have ever loved
would be
sitting
in the desk
right next to me.

Elbow partners.
Soul mates.

One day,
I was going to
show him
one
of my poems.

And not the ones
Mrs. Maldonado
makes us write

to show
we understand
where to break
the line,
where to splice
the comma.

But the ones I write
to show
I don't understand
a thing.

Except, maybe
how to take
ugly things and
make them pretty,
how to scream
with a single word.

How to paint
the face
of a boy
in em dashes
and semicolons
who
doesn't even know
I exist
outside the walls
of this classroom.

In the minutes and seconds and hours
between school days, between class periods.

I thought about taking the poem
and tucking it
under his notebook,
slipping it into his locker,
maybe even

dropping
it in his backpack.

I imagined him finding it there,
reading it,
that goofy smile
on his face,
knowing
from the first
line
that it was my pen,
my bleeding heart on the page.

Me.

But that was six months ago.

Before Mrs. Maldonado
gave me a pass to the office.

Before I saw Papi
still in his coveralls from work

because Mami was
already at the hospital.

Before I saw Grandpa
held
down
by straps,
shivering and
scared.

Before the doctor said the word

dementia.

That was six months ago.

And now I sit
in the far corner
of the room,
tensing
every time
the door opens,
every time
one of the aides
hands Mrs. Maldonado
a note,
every time
she scans
the room,
her eyes
almost
landing
like an X
on my face.

Now my elbow partner is Naomi Duncan,
who tries hard
to make me laugh.

And Yeong Kim
asked
another girl
to homecoming.

A Haiku about Math

Hell is a math class.
We're always solving for X
but no one knows Y.

Rescue

In fourth period
when one of the aides
hands a pass
to Mr. Nguyen
I know
it's for me.

But there are no
heart palpitations
or sweaty palms.

Instead,
I try to hide
my smile
as I pack my things
and head for the hallway.

"Mr. Nguyen
was about to hand out
a pop quiz.
So,
you're welcome."
Victoria
throws an arm around me.

"You're a lifesaver."
I kiss her on the cheek,
grateful she quit
the dance team (the other girls never
let me hang out with them anyway)
and became an office aide.

Aunt Veronica was pissed
and told Victoria
no college
was going to accept her

if she couldn't stick
with something

and Victoria said
college
was *for the birds.*

Something Grandpa
used to say
because,
to him,
classrooms
with four walls
were the worst kind.

Because,
to him,
the best way to learn
was to fall
into the world
head first.

Victoria was grounded
for a whole month.

But here,
on the other side,
she's back
to breaking the rules,
more than happy
to show me how.

I finally ask, "Where to?"

She raises an eyebrow,
the arch perfectly
penciled in.
"Luchas?"

I'm already salivating.
"Luchas."

We skip out
through the side doors,
cross the parking lot,
and hop the chain-link fence.

On the way,
we pass the soccer field
where Javi Montoya,
Victoria's latest crush,
is running
shirtless.

She stares.
We both do.

"When is he finally going to ask you out?" I say.

She gives him a small wave,
her lashes fluttering,
drawing his gaze
like a fish on a hook.

He flops like one too,
losing the ball
while his teammates groan.
Then they spot us,
whistling and hooting
until my skin is on fire

until I like the way it feels.

Victoria looks back one more time
before answering my question.
"I already did."

"Wait.
You asked *him* out?"

"He was taking too long."
She clicks her teeth.
"Now I'm the one in control."

This is the thing about Victoria.
She is always in control.
Even when she's not.

"You're amazing."

"I'm bored."
She takes my hand,
leading us
across the street
while the pedestrian signal
screams red.

Grandpa put Luchas
on the map
with a five-hundred-word
article in the *New York Times*.

He raved about their
adobo recipe,
their pork roasting method,
and coconut horchata,
every word he wrote
settling on the tongue
as if you were eating right next to him.

As we enter, I'm almost
knocked back
by the smell of comino and lime,
the citrus sticking
to the back of my throat.

Victoria and I both reach
to graze the framed article
hanging by the door,
my hand lingering over
the photo of Grandpa
and the owner, Mr. Gomez,
laughing together
over a story
I'll never know.

We order
al pastor tacos,
with cilantro
extra onions
and tomatillo salsa.

Grease and pineapple juice
drip down our faces
while we
laugh
(and almost choke)
as we act out
Victoria's
idea of a
perfect date.

"And then he'll
take my hand across the table,
look into my eyes,
and tell me how in love he is with me."
Victoria beams.

I narrow my eyes at her.
"And you'll say?"

She squeezes my hand
like I'm Javi Montoya,
desperate
and waiting

on the other side
of the table.

"I'll say..."
She stares deep into my eyes.
"I."
She leans across the table.
"Love."
She licks her lips.
"Tacos."

I snort.
She cackles.
Falling over ourselves
at the thought
that anything
could be better
than
the perfect
taco.

Drifting

I try to hold on
to the laughter,
like a tether.

But I feel myself
drifting
farther and farther
away from
reality,
from this body
I don't always hate.

But you should.

Mami's voice
is a flame at the back
of my skull.

The one
she doesn't even
have to use anymore
because
every cell in me
has it memorized.

The one that
whispers praise
for a growling stomach.

The one that
slips over me
like a straitjacket,
squeezing
until I make myself
small.

I go quiet.

It squeezes

and Victoria takes my hand.

Stain

I don't make it
to my room
before Mami sees
me.

"Danna."

I stop
at the sound of her voice,
hoping she doesn't know
about me skipping class;
or hoping that's all there is
for her to fume over.

I draw near.
The temperature spikes.

"Hi, Mami."
I smile
like I'm happy
to see her.

But it makes her brow furrow;
her arms cross.

"What's that?"

She runs a sharp
acrylic fingernail
from the corner
of my mouth
down
to my shirt.

And there
just over my racing heart
is a golden grease stain.

All the evidence she needs
to know
that, unlike Victoria,
I am not in control.

Papi senses
the tension
and it draws him out
of the kitchen.

"Hey, mija."
He is a light
at the end
of the hallway.
"Want to help me with dinner?"

Mami answers
for me.
"She already ate."

Raúl

Spark

My uncle
saves me
from the torture
of riding the bus.

Instead,
he scoops me up
in his old
Chevy pickup truck
and I burn
my hand
on the metal seat belt,
hissing
as I click it in place
before
we drive
to the first client's
house.

He laughs.
"You burn up
those fingers
and I won't
be able to
hide
my imperfections
behind
your playing."

I want to tell him
that my playing

doesn't hide a thing.
But I don't.

Pastors have huge egos
and every single one of them
thinks they can sing.
Even if it sounds
like the second
a wild animal
becomes
roadkill.

It's part of
the perception
that they're
special.
Even though
they are
usually
more flawed
than most.

My mom says
it's because
the Devil
only goes after
righteous men.

He doesn't waste his time
with the average
human.

No,
the fun
is in the fall,
the dragging
someone down
from the
mountaintop.

Satan would know.
He fell farther than anyone.

My uncle's not a bad person.
In fact, he's a really good person
who spends all his time
trying to save people's souls,
to bolster them
in times of need,
to love them
when they
don't know
how to love themselves.

But he also
uses food
to make himself feel
rich. And
he would rather
keep his failing flock
than actually
shepherd them
toward truth.

Which is why
he shouts
about apathy
from the pulpit
but never confronts
anyone to their face.

Still,
he tries.

And he pays me
good money
to help him
help others.

Basically,
we are a human jukebox
and through the power of music,
we lead people
back to the life
they once had.

Alzheimer's patients.
Stroke victims.
People with PTSD.

Anyone who has lost
a piece of themselves,
we try
to help them
get it back.

At first,
I hated
going into strangers' homes.
But now,
I'd do it
even if he didn't pay me.
(I won't tell him that.)

The truth is,
it makes me feel
good
to help people find
the parts of themselves
they thought they'd lost.

Even if it's just
for a second.
Even if it's just
for the length
of a single song.

I like watching
the past

light
behind their eyes
like a match.

Even if the fire
doesn't catch,
even if it's just
a spark,
it makes me hope
that
maybe
someday
I can
find my way back
to the Raúl
I used to be
before
everything
gentle in me
hardened
or hid.

Before I used
my own spark
to set fire
to the things
I used to
love.

Salvage

Mr. Villarreal
is all smiles.
Like he knows
that we're here
to see him
but not that
it's because he's sick
or because his family is desperate
and scared
and all the other
punch-in-the-gut feelings
you have
when someone you love
is dying.

He doesn't know he's dying.

That is the real gift
families give
when they pay us
fifty dollars an hour
for "music therapy."

The illusion is the gift.

The songs about Jesus,
about falling in love,
about the past,
they wrench the sands
back through
the neck
of the hourglass.

While we sing "Amor de Mis Amores,"
I watch it happen.

I strum, my uncle
filling in the words
he can't remember
with quick glances
at his computer.

Mr. Villarreal's eyes light up
as we play his request—
his wife's favorite song.

I can't read music
so I do my best
to remember
how the song sounded
in my grandparents' living
room when they were still
alive.

"Aurora,"
Mr. Villarreal taps his knee,
leading my strumming
as much as my own memory.
"Aurora, you have to come hear this."

He searches the empty hallway,
before looking toward the front door.

She doesn't come
and I suspect
she isn't here.

The only grain of sand
we can't salvage.

"Aurora?"

The song ends,
wrapping us in a silence
that bleeds.

Mr. Villarreal blinks,
the joy slipping
fast from his face,
like he's searching
through fog.

"I'm here, Grandpa."
A girl about my age
walks into the room
and curls up
on the couch next to Mr. Villarreal.

"Danna…"
He pets her hair.
"This is my granddaughter, Danna."

My uncle reaches for her hand.
"Nice to meet you, Danna."

I reach out next. "Raúl."

She touches my hand.
Her cheeks go pink.
"Hi, Raúl."

Mr. Villarreal's Granddaughter

He smooths her hair,
repeating her name
like some part of him knows
she longs to hear it.

She looks up at him,
that longing
sparkling in her eyes
like she's trying
not to cry.

And I wonder
how often
she gets erased
from his memory.

As she finally lets go of my hand,
I wonder
if I'll ever be able
to erase her
from mine.

Mr. Villarreal's Granddaughter
Part Two

Danna picks the next song.
"Es Mi Niña Bonita."

She says,
"It's the song
we danced to
at my quinces,
Grandpa,
do you remember?"

I carefully
pluck the strings
like they're a secret
code
I can crack
with precision.

But I'm also trying
not to stare
at Danna
and the small
grease stain
on her chest
just above
where the shape
of her bra
shows beneath
her shirt.

Mr. Villarreal's Granddaughter
Part Three

A stray note escapes,
my fingers fumbling.

The sharp twang makes everyone jerk.
My uncle gives me a look.
I stare down at my hands.

And this time I feel Danna looking.
Hard.
Like she is drawing a map of me in her mind.

Sweat paints my upper lip
but I can't reach to wipe it away.
I can't look back.
I can't beg her to show me the map,
to tell me where I'm going.

My uncle holds out the last note of the song.
I run my hand down all six strings.
It ends
and I can breathe.

"What else would you like us to play?"
my uncle asks.

Mr. Villarreal blinks,
his knuckles blanched around the edge
of the couch.

He sits up straighter,
urgent,
and I know he is wading
through fog again.

"Where's Aurora?"
He turns to Danna,
stiffens at her closeness.

She is a stranger.

"Grandpa?"
Her voice cracks.

Mr. Mendoza, Danna's father,
comes into the living room.
He grips the towel hanging over his shoulder
like he's waiting
for a mess.

But the wreckage
is in their eyes.

"Danna, I've got a pot on the stove," Mr. Mendoza says.
"Can you keep an eye on it?"

She heads for the kitchen,
disappearing into the fog.

My uncle asks, "What can we do?"

Mr. Mendoza sighs.
"Can we reschedule?"

Danna

The Boy

His hand
is warm.

It sets off an avalanche,
ice caps melting,
the Antarctic shelf
plunging
into the sea.

I see it all
like one of those
National Geographic
documentaries,
the ones that are supposed
to make us
stop and think
about
the end
of the world.

But for some reason
touching his hand
feels like just the tip
of the iceberg.

Touching his hand
feels like the beginning.

Being Left

When Grandpa first got sick
people who'd only existed
on the periphery
of our lives
started bringing us
casseroles.

At first, it was annoying,
Mami making me
stay in my school clothes
in case anyone showed up
unannounced
when all I wanted to do
was take off my bra
and watch TV.

But on Grandpa's worst days
when it felt like
my world was
being torn at the seams,
having a witness
(even if it was just one of Mami's coworkers
who couldn't pronounce my name correctly)
made the entire thing
feel more
survivable.

Soon,
I started hating
the sound of the front door
closing,
people leaving
us alone
while the unknown
grew fangs.

So when I overhear Raúl's uncle ask,
"What can we do?"
my heart leaps
and then wrenches.

Because all they can do is come back.
And in the meantime
all we can do
is wait.

Scared the Entire Way

There's a knock
and I tiptoe toward
the door, pausing when
I see Raúl's outline
on the other side
of the glass.

I ease it open
and he grins.
"Sorry."

There's a beat
of silence
while we stare
at each other.

I feel a drop of sweat
down the back of my neck.

He bites his lip.

My knees almost buckle.

"Sorry," he says
again. "I left my capo
inside."

I blink.

"Small plastic thing.
It clamps down on the
guitar's neck, shortening
all the strings
at the same time
to change the key
that you're playing in

and I don't know
why I'm telling you all
this—"

He smiles.
I smile.

"I'll take a look."

I find Raúl's capo
under the couch.

I hand it to him,
our fingers touching
for half a second.

Another avalanche.

"Thanks," he says
but he doesn't turn to go.

And I'm grateful.
For five more seconds
of not being alone.

For five more seconds
of being seen.

"Well, I better..."
he eases off the first step.

My heart lurches.

"Wait."
I step out onto the porch.
But I don't know what to say.
How to say *I'm scared*.

He stares at me.
Both of us surprised

that I said it
out loud.

I fumble for words
that make sense.

"You and your uncle,
you do this a lot, right?
Help people who are sick?
People like my grandpa?"

He nods.

"How do you do it?" I ask him.
"How do you watch them slip away?"

He takes a step closer,
looking down at me.
"You just do.
Scared
the entire way."

He's Cute

Victoria's phone
rests between us,
her neon green fingernail
scrolling past photos
of streetlights
and guitar strings
and a cloud shaped
like an alligator.

Not much new
over the past two years.
Not since his
eighth-grade graduation,
a woman with his eyes
tugging on the tassel
of his cap,
while he smiles
straight into the camera.

"He seems deep,"
Victoria deadpans.

I snatch the phone,
grateful our chemistry teacher, Mrs. Douglas,
is asleep at her desk
and the inclusion teacher
is helping kids on the other side of the room.

"He's..." I go pink.

Victoria nudges me.
"He's cute.
Where did you say
you met him again?
You better not have gone
to a party without me."

"He works with the pastor
who does Grandpa's music therapy.
And you know
I would never go to a party without you."

Her eyes widen.
"You mean he's a musician?
Ooh, I bet he's sensitive
and more importantly,
good with his hands."

I snort,
"You're so inappropriate."

Then she whispers in my ear,
"What do you call two jalapeños getting it on?"

I squeal at the punch line
and laugh
so loud
Mrs. Douglas
jerks awake,
grasping at her chair
like she's forgotten
what was holding her up.

Everyone else
starts laughing too,
pent-up energy set loose
the second the bell rings.

"So you gonna
ask him out
or what?"
Victoria says
on our way to
Econ.

Like it's easy.
Like she knows he'll say yes.

I hug my textbook.
"So he can
laugh
in my face?"

She stops me
in the middle
of the hallway.
"So he can
see you
the way I do.
So you can learn
to see yourself
that way too."

Being Cousins Is Not Enough

Victoria
is more like
my sister
than my cousin.

We were born
six days
apart,
in the hottest
July on record.

Two bundles
of fire.

If I were a kite
she'd be the string
that ties me down,
and the breeze
that always knows
how to change
my direction
when I'm drifting
too far
into the abyss
that is my
own brain.

She knows
how to hit
the reset button.

With a dirty joke
that I only pretend
to understand
but that has me

cracking
up anyway.

Or with a forged
note to skip
out on last
period
so we can watch
the boys' basketball
practice
through a crack
in the gym door.

We share a love of
nail art,
corgis,
cooking,
K-pop,
and telenovelas,
but her taste
in boys
is questionable.

She likes the
wannabe vaqueros
with giant belt buckles
and cockroach killers,
boot tips curled to
high heaven,
with mustaches
lying
thin and pathetic
over
chapped lips.

When I think
about her kissing
those lips,
I gag.

"It's just because
you've
never been kissed,"
she says,
poking
at the bruise
Yeong Kim
left behind.

The boy I
~~thought~~
hoped
would be my first.

Until he twirled
a girl who
wasn't me
under a sky
of bright white strobe lights
while I watched
from the bleachers,
the mum Papi made me
hanging heavy
from the dress
Mami didn't think
would fit.

Victoria sees it all,
the memory
playing behind my eyes.

"So what if he took
another girl to
homecoming?"
She lifts my chin.
"It's his loss
and Raúl's gain."

"And if Raúl
rejects me too?"

She throws her arms around me
and says, "I choose you, Danna."

That's why we're sisters.
Because being cousins is not enough.
Because I choose
to love her more deeply
than that.
And because even
when my insides
are scrambled,
the rest of me
sinking
fast,
she chooses
to love me back.

She *always* loves me back.

Granddaughters

When Papi and I
arrived
at the hospital
that day,
the first person
I saw
was Victoria.

In a crop top,
purple lipstick, and gold hoops,
mascara running
down her cheeks.

When she saw me,
she sat up straight,
scraped at her face
and smeared
the evidence
of her softness
across her jeans.

Then she reached for me,
making room
for my tears;
pausing the storm
inside her so
the storm
in me could
break.

I flooded us both
but she didn't
let me
drown.

"It's going to be okay,"
she said,

taking control;
rewiring me
with the sound of
her voice.

Even now,
I can't fall asleep
without calling her first,
without reading her
my lists,
my plans;
her listening
without judgment.

"It's going to be okay," she always says,
before clicking her teeth
and reciting some joke
she saw online.

"Why does a mermaid wear seashells?"
She always pauses for effect.
"Because she outgrew
her B-shells!"

Laughter is our love language
and every time
I'm doubled over
trying to muffle
the sound
in my pillow,
what washes over me
most
is the truth.

Not that everything is going to be okay.
But that even when it's not,
I am not alone.

In the fear
and the sadness
of losing someone,
of never being kissed,
of growing up,
I am not alone.

Raúl

Ghosts

Mr. Lim
likes listening
to sad country songs
while sucking on ginger candy.

The taste
opens him wide enough
for the sound to puncture holes,
memories sprouting like seedlings.

They are bright and colorful
and watching him remember
is like watching a rainbow peek through
the clouds.

"I printed a copy of the words," my uncle says,
sliding the sheet music into Mr. Lim's open hand.
"So you can sing along."

Mr. Lim had a stroke
that stole not just one language,
but three.

English,
Vietnamese,
and Mandarin.

But the words aren't completely gone
because the brain
has two sides.

Two parts of a whole.

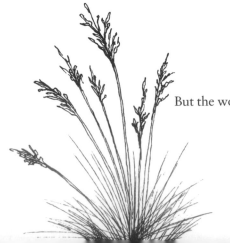

When Mr. Lim sings
he's teaching
the right side of his brain
to make up for what
the left side can't do anymore.

Teaching himself
to adapt.

And the music
is the key,
unlocking the language
and leading it
to his lips.

So he can sing
Johnny Cash
songs
with his whole
body,
reviving
ghosts
that cover me
in goose bumps.

The force of his voice
driving back
the demons
and the hell where they live,
like every bone
is screaming,
*You will not
take me.*

*You will not
take me
yet.*

Alone

"I'm going to make
some rounds
at the hospital,"
my uncle says.
"There's
leftovers
in the fridge."

I lock the door behind him.

The house sighs.
All the air sucked out.
Like the living
was all that propped it up.

But that's not
what I'm doing here.
I don't know
what I'm doing here.

Eat.
Sleep.
Repeat.

Fueling a ghost
who is failing
chemistry.

Around me
the quiet throbs,
a bruise.

Some nights,
I press at the pain,
see how long I can go

before the tenderness
turns numb.

But tonight,
Mr. Lim's voice
fresh in my mind,
I want to fight back,
to force the feelings
into words.

I grip
the neck
of my guitar
and pick at the
wound,
coaxing out
the poison.

A fraught melody,
hand falling
across the strings.

Then
I take a deep breath,
setting loose
the sound
of my own voice.

The house
flinches.

Paper Cuts

When the phone
rings,
my stomach
becomes
a tight fist.

I used to wait
on the
edge
of my bed,
for the sound.

For the sharp
trill
to snake down
the hallway
and hook me.

For the sound
of her voice
on the other
end.

Now,
it grates
on me,
leaving
marks,
paper cuts
I didn't notice
until the days
became months,
became years.

Now those cuts
sting.

Every time
I feel even an ounce
of something,
anything,
they
split;
they
scream.

Because waiting
hurts.

"It hurts,"
I barely breathe
against the
mouthpiece,
finally saying
what I've
only told
my pillow.

Finally
telling
the truth.

"Mom,"
I say, "it
hurts."

"I know," she says.

"But it's over," she says.

"Raúl…"
her voice is
clipped,
turning those paper cuts
into full moons.

"I'm coming
home."

And the fist
unclenches,
for the first
time in
two years,
hope unfurling
with every finger,
the ache
of longing
finally
letting go.

Hope

The fork shakes in my hand.
"Did you know?"

My uncle sits back in his chair,
his plate empty.
"I prayed."

"But did you *know*?"

"We've been trying to appeal
the conviction since your mother
first went in. I knew her lawyer
was making progress but
there were no guarantees.

I didn't want you to get your hopes up."

That is the tremor
running from arm to elbow,
from the soles of my feet
to the tip of my scalp.

Hope.

And it doesn't feel like I thought it would.

Warm.
Safe.

It feels fragile

like a bird I'm clutching too tightly,
wings twitching
like all it wants to do
is leap
from my grasp.

Tomorrow

Tonight
I fight
sleep.

My thoughts
like one of those prank birthday candles
that you can never quite blow out,
shadows and light
flickering across the walls of my mind.

Illuminating my mother's face.

Rising like the sun over
Danna Mendoza.

And back again.

And the hours between midnight
and 7:00 AM
have never felt so
stretched;
the morning
has never felt so
beckoning.

The future has never felt
so
bright.

Danna

The Way to a Man's Heart

After dinner (which Papi actually
lets me eat, despite
Mami's glares)
I pull the small jewelry box
out from under my bed
and rifle through
my grandmother's
old recipe cards.

She and Grandpa met at church.

On the night of the annual fish fry
my grandmother was sitting across the room
at a table with her friends.
Grandpa was sitting with his family,
supposedly just visiting.

The food
was a family-style potluck.

My grandmother brought the chorreadas de piloncillo
and when Grandpa
took a bite
he knew
that the woman who made them
was his
soulmate.

I find the card,
tracing the words.

It still smells like cinnamon.

I Wish She Didn't Know

Mrs. Baker calls me in
first thing.

I had barely gotten my favorite pink flair pen out of my bag
before she showed up at Mr. Núñez's classroom door.
(She knows not to send a pass
or else I might have an anxiety attack,
imagining Grandpa
getting hurt
or lost
or worse.)

Sometimes I wish she didn't know me so well;
that she hadn't learned my deepest darkest
fears. Or how
they show up unannounced
under the most mundane circumstances.

I wish she didn't know about what happened six months ago.

Or why I wear a jacket to school
even when it's hot out
in case my clothes cling too tightly
to the parts of my body
Mami hates most.

Mrs. Baker knows about
the diets and the scale Mami put in my bathroom
and that I prefer to cry
in the shower because if I pretend hard enough
it's like I'm not really crying at all.

She knows about all of that
because when she called me into her office
to ask about my grandpa and whether or not
his illness was affecting my grades,

I opened my mouth to answer
and truths I didn't even know I'd been choking on
fell out.

Now she keeps a close eye on me
always
and she has started to catch on
to Victoria's and my little midday excursions.

"Where were you?"
She gets straight to the point
because she knows I'm as good as
any poet
at twisting words
into truth.

"I was off campus
for an important meeting."

Mrs. Baker
raises an eyebrow.

I smile,
my father's smile—
the only thing in the world
that is powerful
enough to disarm my mother.

It works on Mrs. Baker too.

She sighs.
"Fine. You don't have to tell me where you were.
But I'm sure your parents will want to know.
I just sent them an email about your
lunch detention tomorrow."

Our Little Secret

Papi is waiting at the kitchen table when I get home.

In front of him
is a plate of marranitos
still warm from the oven.

"Siéntate," he says.

Spanish is Papi's love language,
used in joy, passion, and the mild fuming he calls anger.
(Because who gets angry and bakes cookies?)

"¿Tienes algo que decirme?"

I stare at the plate of cookies.
"These smell delicious."

"Nah-uh." He wags a finger.
"These are bait."

I cross my arms.
"Too bad I'm not a fish."

"Well, your mother is going to gut you
like one if she finds out you've been skipping class."

This time I raise an eyebrow.
"If?"

He sighs, staring
at me long and hard
like he's looking for
the answers to all the hard
questions.

I almost ask him
what he sees. If

I hold any wisdom
in this body
that is half him
and half
her.

If there's any proof
it's actually
good
for something
other than scolding.

But Papi doesn't scold me.

He hands me a cookie.

"If I tell her,
which I haven't decided
to do
yet."

I take a bite, a shock
of cinnamon. "Why
not?"

"Because your mother is already dealing with a lot right
        now.
She's working more hours so your grandpa can get music
        therapy twice a week.
She's having trouble sleeping.
And I think she's scared."

I wrinkle my nose.
"Mami doesn't get scared."
She gets angry.

"You don't know her as well as you think you do."
Papi bites the head off one of the marranitos.

"I'm not going to tell her because I don't want to add to her
     stress.
But that doesn't mean you're not going to be punished."

When I was little,
before Mami would get me
with la pela,
Papi would wedge himself
into the corner,
looking on as he said,
"This is going to hurt us
a lot more than it's going to hurt you."

Mami would spank me
and as my eyes filled with tears
so would his.

So I know whatever's coming now
is not going to hurt me
as much as it hurts him.

But then he says, "You're grounded
for two weeks
and you're going to help me
clean out the attic."

And the sting is immediate.
Cookie tumbles
out of my mouth.

"Be careful," Papi says,
"you're going to catch
flies."

Lunch Detention

I don't know why
kids are so scared
of lunch detention.

My anxiety
sits at a level ten
most days
and yet, even I know
lunch detention
is the teen version
of nap time.

I walk in just as the bell rings
and the regulars are already snoring,
legs spread wide under their desks,
arms folded into pillows.

Nothing menacing at all.

Just a bunch of kids
who were probably tardy
to class too many times
because they were up late,
working, or babysitting, or worrying
about things
adults never care enough
to ask about.

Andrea Meyer,
in the front row,
has a two-year-old
and a part-time job
at Burger King.

Sean Le,
sitting behind her,

works at his parents'
laundromat
every day after school.

Nate Burgess,
in the corner,
rides his bike to school
in the rain,
his little brother
sitting on the handlebars
wrapped in both their coats,
because they live
just outside the bus route.

When you skip class,
as is now part of my regular routine,
you start to notice other people's
routines too.

Like how Andrea always sneaks into the
girls' locker room
to change into her uniform
before the last bell,
or how Sean
becomes a salesman
every time there's a substitute,
slipping them his parents' business card
on his way out the door,
or how Nate
stops by the cafeteria
every Friday afternoon
to pick up a sack of food
for him and his brother
to eat
over the weekend.

When you're hiding
in places you're not supposed
to be,

you notice lots of things
you're not supposed
to see.

Things that remind you
that lunch detention
isn't actually
nap time for teens,
but
the Island of Misfit Toys.

The overstuffed coat closet
where your mother shoves
all the things
she doesn't have
a place for.

The solution
to a problem
people don't actually
want to solve.

Sorpresa

When Papi tries out a new recipe
he always makes me
close my eyes
before leading
the food
to my mouth.

As I bite down
he says
with the giddiness of a kid
on Christmas morning,
"¡Sorpresa!"

And he is always right.

I am never expecting
what comes next:
the shot of citrus
or the jolt of heat
or the bittersweet explosion
on my tongue.

And every time I open my eyes
he is smiling
so wide,
crooked teeth and gums showing,
and I laugh,
almost choking
at the sight of someone
so embarrassingly goofy,
so absolutely
full
of love.

When life yells,
"¡Sorpresa!"

I cower
and brace
for pain.

But when Papi says it
I trust
and wait
for joy.

One minute before the end of lunch detention,
I reach into my bag
and grab the Tupperware container
of chorreadas de piloncillo.

My second test batch,
still slightly warm.

Then I place a cookie
on the corner of each desk
just as the bell
screams
that nap time
is over.

Andrea raises her head.
Sean scrubs his eyes.
Nate lets out a wide yawn.

And then they see
the cookies,
la sorpresa
on their faces
slapping me with Papi's goofy grin,
which I hide
behind my notebook
on my way out the door.

Raúl

She Tried

When I was a kid,
and my mom was still around,
she gave me everything
I ever wanted.

Everything I needed.

Except a father.

And God knows she tried.

With the landlord
and my soccer coach
and strangers who were never around long enough
for me to learn their names.

Mom tried
to make a family
like the ones on TV.

Mom tried.

For me.

And one day
that trying led her to
him.

He didn't like me
from the start.

Like he could already see
the man

trapped beneath
my fourteen-year-old skin.

Trying to punch his way out.

He punched first,
leaving me with a bloody nose
one night when he was drunk,
when Mom was working late,
when there was no one around
to hear me cry.

All the proof he needed
that I wasn't a man
yet
that I still bruised
easy
that I still
needed
my mother.

But he didn't notice.

She didn't either.
She was too busy trying.

Trying to be perfect.
Trying to make him happy.
Trying to make him stay.

Favors soon became commands.
Then those commands became
sirens and flashing lights;
my mother's face in the back of a police car;
leaving me
with bruises so deep
not even shedding my fourteen-year-old skin
could get rid of them.

My mom had never even touched drugs,
hadn't gotten hooked on them
like Manny's mother did,
hadn't even known
that's what was in the package
her boyfriend asked her to deliver
for him.

Until the cops showed up.

And I tried to tell them.
With my fourteen-year-old voice
in my fourteen-year-old body
that had never wanted
anything more
than to shed that skin,
to grow into a man
so I could protect her.

But I couldn't.

I couldn't protect her.

Coming Home

My uncle lets me stay home
from school.

It's a long drive to the prison
and he doesn't want to go alone.

I wouldn't have let him
go without me anyway.

I want to be the one
to carry her stuff
and put it in the car.

I want to
buckle her
into the front seat.

I want to hear her breathing
as we drive away
from the barbed wire fence.

I want to see with my eyes
and ears
and hands
that she's coming home.

Dancing

I catch sight of her shoulder
through the small glass window
as they lead her toward
the exit.

I stop breathing
for three whole seconds.

A buzzer sounds.
The door unlocks.
Mom steps through.

And she is smiling
with her whole body,
arms outstretched,
reaching for me.

"Raúl.Raúl.Raúl.Raúl."

She rocks me
like a baby
and I let her,
the two of us
so big,
it's more like dancing.

Like there is music
in our souls
for the first time
in a long time.

Like our bodies are finally free.

Stretched

Before they took her,
Mom and I used to live
in a small apartment on
the other side of town.

We only went to Uncle Mario's
on holidays.

As I lead Mom over the threshold,
I wonder if it feels like Christmas.
I wonder if she feels anything at all.

She was quiet on the drive,
the three hours
chopped up
by my uncle's attempts
at small talk.

"Mrs. Mondragon
said she can't wait to see you."

"Mr. Solis
got married last week."

"Doña Fernanda
started dialysis over the summer."

"The congregation
has doubled in size
since you were last there."

She cast her voice to the back seat—
"How are you doing in school,
Raúl?"—ignoring
Uncle Mario's musings.

And it felt like we were
still stretched
between phone lines,
miles
and
miles
between us.

Warmer

Dinner is warmer,
Mom kneading me like dough,
mussing my hair,
and covering me in
long kisses that don't want to let go.

"You're so tall now, mijito.
I was so worried
you'd end up short
like me."

She grabs me
by the cheek.
"I was so worried."
And her eyes still well up with it.

"I'm fine, Mom.
We were worried about you."

For the first time all night
she takes her eyes off me.

The warmth
snuffed out
cold.

Like I accidentally
put a crack
in the past,
letting it seep in
to the now.

"Don't worry about me, mijito."
She gets up from the table,
eyes still down.
"I'm just tired."

Awake

Light bleeds beneath the doorframe.

It's 1:00 AM.

I thought that once
she was home,
once I knew
that she was just on the other side
of the wall,
that she was safe,
I'd finally be able to sleep.

But instead,
I'm staring at the light,
eyes red
head pounding hard as ever
because she isn't sleeping either.

I creep into the hallway
and make my way
to her door.

On the other side,
she sniffs.

"Mom?"

I ease the door open
but she's not in bed.

She's sitting by the window
watching the moon.

"Come here, mijito."

She beckons me
like I should hurry.

Like there is something
outside
being born.

Then she points at the moon
and I see.

It is smiling.

Danna

Where Mami Used to Dream

The attic
is unbearably hot.
Like stepping into someone's open mouth
right after they've eaten dirt.

I scrape my finger
across an old shelf
and it comes back
covered in dust.

If I hold my breath,
I can almost pretend
we're standing inside
a snow globe
instead
of the place
where Mami used to
dream.

One of her easels sits
angled in the light
shining through
the open window.

It cuts across the floor,
landing at my feet.

When I was little,
I wasn't allowed to watch her
work.

I touched too many things.
Made too many messes.
Asked too many questions.

Like,
"What's that, Mami?"
"What are you drawing, Mami?"
"Can I help you, Mami?"
"Why won't you play with me, Mami?"

"That's not a toy," she'd snap.
"Put that down."
"Let go."
"Did you hear what I just said?"
"Get out!"

Papi would lead me by the hand
to the kitchen
before plopping me onto a stool.

Then he'd dump flour onto the countertop
and let me play
with leftover dough.
Or he'd help me hold the mixer
while we whipped some heavy cream.

The mess
on our faces and hands.
The best feeling
in the world.

"We have to clean this up before Mami sees,"
I'd say,
joy and panic like two
frantic butterflies
between my ribs.

Then he'd dab
a dollop
of icing on my nose.
"Life is messy, mija."
He'd sigh.
"No matter how much
people try to pretend like it's not."

Then...

upstairs,
we'd hear
the slice of paper,
tin hitting the hardwood floor,
Mami
ripping
her painting
in half

because
the dream was better.

The dream was always better.

Deep Down

"Your mother thinks we're just cleaning up
the mess,
taking something
off her to-do list."

"But...?"
I cross my arms
over my paint-splattered
Adventure Time T-shirt
that I always wear
when it's my turn
to clean the bathrooms.

"But..."
Papi smiles so wide
and I know in an instant
that he's going to get
his heart broken.

It happens every Christmas
every Valentine's Day
every wedding anniversary.

Papi tries.
With flowers, and candy, and jewelry, and a new camera, and
        a fancy purse.

When it comes to Mami,
Papi doesn't *stop* trying.

So even though
my stomach knots
with pity,
when his mouth says, "We're
going to give her a real studio,"
and his eyes say, *a place*

to dream again,
I don't tell him that it's pointless
or stupid
or any of the other things
anger tries
to force to my lips.

I only nod
and smile back
because deep down
there is a part of me
that hopes.

That can't stop trying either.

To bring her dreams to life
even if I wasn't one of them.

The Princess in the Tower

Papi shoves some boxes
to one side of the room,
clearing the floor
before handing me a broom.

"Remember when you used to pretend
this was your knight in shining armor?"

I take a long step, twirling the broom
like we're dancing.

Then I sneak up on Papi,
pretending to jab it
through his gut.

"Mostly it was a sword."

He clutches his stomach,
staggering back, and gagging
like he's choking on his own blood.

"That's right."
He laughs.
"You were always up here
slaying dragons,
rescuing your mother
like she was a princess
locked up
in a tower."

I kneel, sweeping dirt
into the dustpan.

Remembering.

She wasn't the princess,
I want to tell him.

She was *never* the princess.

She was the dragon.

Monsters

When Mami wasn't home,
I would climb the stairs,
pretending to be a valiant knight.

I would reach the door,
mark myself with the sign
of the cross,
and then unsheathe my sword
before stepping inside.

The shadows hid
goblins and trolls,
fanged monsters and ghosts;
sometimes aliens too.

Mrs. Maldonado would call them
metaphors.

Symbols
for Mami's coldness.
Her criticism.

Everything about her
that made me shrivel
and hide.

I didn't know that then.

All I knew was that
standing in her
space
made the hairs on my arms
stand on end.

That being that close to her
was thrilling
and terrifying.

That the terror
weakened
with each monster
I slayed.

So I slayed them all,
before tiptoeing
to her latest painting,
always a portrait,
always a pair of eyes
that made me ache.

Entire worlds,
glassy and glistening
like they were holding back tears.

A consequence of being
too wide open.
Like they'd seen too much.

Now I know
those eyes weren't a stranger's.

They stung
because
they were Mami's.

The way she was
when she first saw
all those monsters
I was always trying to slay.

Up close.

Mami was a girl once.

Mami was *me*
once.

That's what Papi says.

That's what Grandpa used to say too.

And Grandma Aurora before she died.

They told me
who my mother
used to be

so I would love her
enough
for the both of us.

In the flashes of sunlight,
I still see those eyes.

Wide open.

A warning.

That sometimes life
leaves a mark.

That sometimes,
even when we think
we've cleaned things up,
that we've made things right,
we are still
stained.

Papi puts a hand on my shoulder.
"After we slap some paint on it,
maybe it won't be so scary
anymore."
He gives me
a sad smile.
"For either of you."

Trying, Trying, Trying

Four hours later and it finally
stops snowing
in the attic.

Instead,
the dust is on our clothes,
in our hair,
smeared with sweat
across our faces.

I feel disgusting.

"Does this mean
I'm not grounded
anymore?" I sweep the last
of the dirt and debris
into the trash bag
Papi is holding.

"We'll see..."
He ties up the bag,
one eye on me
like I'm still not
to be trusted.
"You can have your phone back.
But part two of this renovation
starts Saturday morning at 9:00 AM."

"Nine?"
I cross my arms.
"In the *morning*?"

He crosses his arms in response.
"And if you skip class again
it'll be six."

"Why don't we just finish
right now? I'm already
covered in filth."

"Because your grandpa's music therapy
starts in..."

The doorbell rings,
the sound sharp
and piercing straight
through me.

"Well, it starts right now."
Papi heads downstairs.

My heart pounds,
new sweat
tracing chalk lines
down my face.

My face.

It's covered in twelve layers of dust.
But even that
isn't thick enough
to hide the mustache
I just didn't feel
like shaving this morning.

Or the zit on my nose
that is so red
it looks angry.

Suddenly,
I'm standing inches
from the window.

The one Mami used to stare out
while she painted

faces with perfect skin,
pointed chins,
smooth long necks.

I stare at my reflection.
Round in all the wrong places.
Pocked with imperfections.

And I don't always see them.
Sometimes when Victoria
is making me laugh
or when I catch
my reflection in the sheen
of my favorite cutting knife,
I think I'm beautiful.

But if your own mother doesn't agree,
can it still be true?

I don't want to.
But
I look closer.

At every inch.

And suddenly,
I understand why,
after hours of painting,
after hours of *trying,*
trying, trying
to make something beautiful
Mami's portraits would end up
in tatters on the floor.

Beautiful

I hear Raúl tuning his guitar
and I know I have exactly forty-five minutes
to make my move.

I jump in the shower and scrub
like my life depends on it.

I tie my wet hair in a knot.

I douse myself in Mami's perfume.

Then I run.

Down the stairs,
into the kitchen,
before rummaging through
the pantry.

I grab ingredients by the armful,
pouring and mixing by memory,
remembering every tweak
from every test batch.

Praying
as I scoop dough
and load the cookies
into the oven
for a bit
of Aurora's stardust
to sprinkle down
and bless me.

The oven dings and I jump.

"What's going on in here?"
Papi gestures to the countertop,

to the mess that is almost as bad
as the one we just finished cleaning up.

"I'll take care of it."
I wipe everything down
while the cookies cool.

When Papi reaches for one,
I don't think
before I slap his hand away.

He gasps.

"I'm sorry."
I'm sweating again.
"Those are for..."

I can't speak
and Papi follows my eyes
to the living room,
to Raúl's head
where it peeks over the couch.

Papi smiles, and I relent,
letting him take a cookie
from my tray. Then he closes
his eyes, holding the flavors
in his mouth.

I hold my breath,
waiting for him to tell me my fate.

He groans. "Delicioso, mija.
He's going to love them."

My face feels like it's on fire.

When I hear Raúl
snapping the locks closed

on his guitar case,
the fire spreads,
sparking in my belly,
in the tips of my fingers.

I arrange the cookies
on a plate,
soft and golden-brown;
the pecans nestled
in the dough,
speckled with cinnamon
like constellations.

They look beautiful.

Before Raúl reaches the door,
I hold the cookies out to him.
"These
are for
you."

He looks at the cookies.

He looks at me.

He smiles
and I see
that his bottom teeth
are crooked
like Papi's.

"Thank you," he says.

He takes the cookies
and as he leaves,
I see
that his face is on fire too.

I Did It

Victoria answers on the first ring.
"You're free!"

"I'm exhausted."
I flop down onto my bed,
replaying the look
on Raúl's face,
the sound of his voice.

The surprise.
Like the cookies were
something special.

"Raúl and his uncle came back
for Grandpa's music therapy."

"And...?"

"I gave him Grandma's
chorreadas de piloncillo."

She gasps.
"Danna."

My cheeks burn.
"What?"

"Those are engagement cookies."

My heart pounds.
"I'm not trying to get engaged.
I just want..."

"Mm-hmm." I hear her smile
through the phone.
"You just want what?"

"I don't know."
I roll face-first
into my pillow
and squeal.

"You do."
Victoria's voice
is suddenly serious.
"You were brave today,
Danna.
Now, get your mom's
voice out of your head
and tell me what you want."

The truth
blooms
like a flower
poking up
through soil.

Reaching
for the sun.

"I want him to be my boyfriend."

"And with the curse
you put on those cookies,
he will."

Raúl

Fireworks

The cookies
are warm in my lap.

I cradle them
like something fragile.

When Danna handed them to me,
that's how I felt.

Exposed.
Breakable.

Like the cookies were
an olive branch
trying to coax me back
into my human skin.

For so long,
I've just been wearing it.
Like a coat
that doesn't quite
fit.

But when Danna looks at me
she doesn't seem to see
a ghost.

I don't wait,
taking a bite of one of the cookies
as we pull into a gas station.

"You gonna share
or what?" Uncle Mario
takes one.

As the cookie
crumbles,
falling apart
in our mouths,
sparks of cinnamon
landing on our tongues
like fireworks,
my uncle shakes his head.

"Oh no."
Then he smiles.
"I think she's in love with you, kid."

And I didn't know
love even had a taste.
I didn't know
you could see it
glittering in the crust
of a cookie.

But as it rests on my tongue,
as I swallow it
down,
as it strikes my heart
on the way,
ringing it like a bell,
I feel
my mother and I
dancing;
I feel
myself
cradling my guitar.

I feel
my heart.

Stretched.
Wide open.
Awake.

Olive Branch

Mom is on the couch
when we walk through the door,
wrapped in a thin blanket,
curled up tight
like she's afraid
of falling off the edge.

She looks up at the sound
of Uncle Mario tossing his keys
on the kitchen table.

"I'm sorry,"
he says
like he's talking to
one of the old people
we work with
who have forgotten
where they are.

But Mom isn't forgetting.

I can tell by the look in her eyes
as she scans us up and down;
as she stares at the plate of cookies
I'm holding,
that she is remembering.

That those memories
are heavy
like chains.

That she is sinking.

I sit down next to her
and hold out the plate of cookies.

An olive branch,
coaxing her back
into her human skin.

She smiles,
takes a bite of one,
eyes lit up
like she's remembering
something new.

That she is safe.
That she is home.

And I wonder if she tastes the love.
If she thinks I put it there
even though I could never
in a million years
make something
quite as good.

Girlfriend

"How often does
does your uncle stop
at the bakery?" Mom asks.
"He's going to give himself
diabetes."

"I'm healthy as a horse,"
Uncle Mario says.
Then he grins
wide. "Actually,
they're from Raúl's
secret admirer."

Mom pinches the fat
on my hip. "You've
got a girlfriend?"

"Ouch." I widen my eyes
at Uncle Mario. Then turn
to Mom. "She was just being
nice."

"Nice…"
Mom's right eyebrow
is like the taut string
on a bow and arrow.
"What's her name?"

"Danna." I stuff another cookie
in my mouth, trying to avoid more questions.

"Danna Mendoza Villarreal." Uncle Mario adds,
"She's the granddaughter of one of our
new clients. Same age as Raúl. Very pretty girl."

"And how old are you, Raúl?"
Mom crosses her arms.

"Uh, I'm sixteen."

"Exactly."
Her voice is stern, suspicious.
"You are only sixteen.
Too young to have a girlfriend.
Too young to care about anything
but school. Do you understand?"

I nod,
remembering what it feels like
to be scolded. To be told what to do.

And it's like she's taken those chains
that were holding her down
for so long
and she's tied them around me
instead.

Good Enough

Manny spins his drumsticks
while my uncle
tells the praise band
that they sound amazing.

"But could you hold the microphone
a few inches away from your mouth, Betsy?"

"And could you watch Manny count you in
at the beginning of each song, Jorge?"

"And, Virginia, could you practice that solo
a little more over the weekend?"

"But overall, you guys sounded great!"

Lies.

Pastors tell them all the time,
which is why Virginia doesn't even bat an eye
and Jorge just nods and smiles
and Betsy is busy looking at her phone.

Because he told them they were good
and what they heard
is that they're good enough.

And if an alien came down to Earth
and asked me
what a Christian is,
that's what I would tell them.

That it's a person who thinks
they're good enough.

Because they go to church.
Because they believe in God.
Because they tithe and volunteer in the praise band or
the children's church.

Serving the Lord
in ways
that keep their hands clean.

That give them
the keys to heaven
without walking through
hell first.

Even though,
anyone who's half awake
during Uncle Mario's sermons
would know that
that's where Jesus lives.

In the muck.
In the dark.
In the places where faith is all you have.

But what kind of God is that?
A God that descends
into the deepest, darkest places
who would rather sit
and hold your hand
than offer you a ladder
to climb your way out.

Jackpot

"Hey, Raúl, why don't you invite Danna
to church on Sunday?"

Uncle Mario lobs the question
right in front of Manny
who he knows gossips as much
as the viejitas who spend
their Saturday nights knitting
caps for the homeless
as an excuse to talk shit
about the other people at church.

Uncle Mario complains about low membership
but when the welcoming committee
is a bunch of wolves in sheep's clothing,
it's no wonder people don't come back.

Who likes being sprinkled with holy water
and then called a puta on their way to the pew?

This time
Manny is looking at me
like I'm the puto.

"Whoa, whoa, whoa."
He jumps out from behind his drum set.
"*Who* is Danna?"

"No one," I say,
shooting daggers at Uncle Mario
as he walks back to his office.

"Obviously not."
He shakes my shoulder.
"Dude, your face is burning up."

I shrug him off
but I know he's not going to
let this go until I give him something.

"Uncle Mario and I
are working with her grandfather.
He's got dementia."

"Oh, that sucks."
Manny sits down beside me.
"Well, is she hot?"

I shake my head, annoyed.
"I don't know."

"You look like a fucking tomato.
She's definitely hot."
He nudges me.
"You got her picture in your phone?"

"I don't even have her number."

"What?" He smacks me.
"Dude, you've got no game."
He grabs my phone out of my hand.
"What's her last name?"

Part of me doesn't want to tell him.
Giving Manny her personal information
feels a little like feeding her to a shark.
Maybe me too.

But
Manny has the best social sleuthing skills
I've ever seen and deep down in the places
that are currently turning me into
a human tomato,
all I want is to know everything
about her I possibly can.

"Mendoza Villarreal."

He types it in
and her Instagram pops up first.

He wriggles his eyebrows,
scrolling.
"Jackpot."

Does She Have a Sister?

Most of the pictures are of food—
beignets from Baton Creole, ice cream from
Michoacana,
elote from Vámonos, a bacon cheeseburger from
Billy's.

Manny groans. "Oh no,
she's one of those."
He scrolls faster.
"Show us your face!"

And then there it is.
Up close, the warm
color of coffee,
lips pink like she's
just eaten a piece of candy.

"Oh, *hello*..."
Manny's eyes widen.
"She's cute, dude."
He smacks me again,
this time more gentle.
"You did good, kid."

"I didn't *do* anything.
She just made me some cookies,
that's all."

"She made you *cookies*?"
He bites his knuckles.
"Damn, Raúl.
Cute, made the first move, *and*
she can bake? That's some wifey shit
right there."

My mother's voice
bangs around

inside my head.
"We're sixteen.
I'm not looking for a wifey."

"Maybe you're not looking for a wife."
He holds the phone up.
"But she's *definitely* looking for you."

My face is the sun again,
burning in the best way.

Manny scrolls through more photos,
pausing to ooh and ahh at each one
like an old borracho
yelling "mamacita"
at women just trying to cross the street.

Then his face lights up.
"Hey, man,
do you think she has
a sister?"

Push Send

Manny opens a DM
and my heart shoots
into my throat.

"Wait,
what are you doing?"

He pats me on the shoulder.
"Helping you."

"I don't need— "

Hey girl.

"No."

He tries again.

Sup?

I shake my head.
"Are you kidding me?"

"Okay, okay,
what about...?"
He types,

Hi

"That's creepier
than the other two combined."

" 'Hi'?"
He furrows his brow,
leans back
like I'm from

another planet.
" 'Hi' is creepy?"

"Give me that."
I take the phone
and it feels like
I'm floating,
out of my body,
out of my mind
with fear.

What if she thinks I'm a loser?
What if she's changed her mind?
What if the cookies actually meant nothing?

But...

What if she *likes* me?

What if I like her too?

I bite my lip,
until it hurts
too much
not to push
Send.

Danna

No Cookies for Breakfast

I lied to Papi
when I told him
all the cookies
were for Raúl.

The truth is,
I saved a few
for Grandpa.

Another test
like the coffee
and the chiles en nogada
and everything else we've tried
to help him remember.

Those tastes were attached to memories.
These cookies are
bits of my grandmother's
soul.

Mami isn't awake yet
and I can hear Papi
in the bathroom
still shaving.

I sit next to Grandpa's bed.
I place the plate of cookies on the mattress.

"I made these for you, Grandpa."

He smiles but it's confused.
Maybe because I'm trying to feed him

cookies for breakfast
or because he doesn't know how
this strange girl got in his room.

I smile back,
trying to be gentle,
to be patient,
to coax him out of the
dark cave where he lives.

"They're chorreadas de piloncillo."

His eyes brighten.

He reaches for one.

Then he takes a bite,
breathing deep through his nose
like he's afraid of letting the flavors escape.

"They're delicious, mija."
He holds my cheek in his hand.
"But you know your grandmother
doesn't let us eat cookies
for breakfast."

Did I Ever Tell You?

He takes another cookie,
a mischievous twinkle
in his eye
like he knows
my grandmother Aurora
might come in any minute
and find us
breaking the rules.

I don't tell him we're safe.
That she'll never find us here.

Instead, I keep my mouth shut.

I listen.

He taps my nose.
"Did I ever tell you
about the first time
I ever laid eyes
on your grandmother?"

I smile, letting him
get lost,
letting myself
get lost too.

"She thinks the first time I saw her
was at the fish fry.
She thinks I fell in love with her
when I took a bite of one of these cookies.

"But
I fell in love with her
three months before
when I saw her selling

vegetables at her father's
produce stand.

"Her hair was tied back with a bandanna
and her face was sunburnt from
hoeing all week;
looked like she had on her brother's jeans.
They were oil-stained
and covered in dirt.
She was washing the lettuce
off with a hose.

"Never saw me.
Barely even looked up
from where she was working.

"But eventually,
she stood up straight,
wiped the sweat from her brow,
staring into the sun
like she was challenging it
to a duel.

"And I thought,
That is the most beautiful
woman I have ever
seen."

Thirty-Seven Minutes

He remembers
for thirty-seven minutes.

Just.
Minutes.

Just long enough
for us to share
three cookies.

He cracked
the last one
in half
and handed
the bigger half to me.

I ate it slowly,
feeling time
dissolve.

I didn't know my great-grandfather
owned a produce stand.

I didn't know Grandpa
had fallen in love with my grandmother
after seeing her there
washing lettuce
by the side of the road.

I didn't know
there was so much
I didn't know.

But before I could ask him
what else
he'd never told me,

the monster
dragged him back
inside the cave.

I lost him.
Again.

The memories
like rot in my mouth
because I knew
it wouldn't be the last time
I'd lose him
until
it
was...

Hey

My phone dings,
still warm from the
twenty-seven texts
Victoria just sent me
of photos of potential outfits
for her date with Javi.

He's taking her
axe-throwing
(her idea)
and then
somewhere secret
that requires
shoes
she doesn't mind
getting wet.

Apparently
he's been working
extra shifts
at his family's restaurant
to save up.

I suspect
paddleboats,
the two of them
kissing under the stars
while a warm breeze
blows off the lake.

Envy sinks its teeth in me.

I bite the inside
of my cheek,
pushing it away.

Then I spot the new DM
in my inbox
from an account with a
metal sugar skull
as the profile photo.

I open the message.
My thoughts turn
to static.

Raúl.

The message is from Raúl.

> Hey, Danna.
> Just wanted to say thanks again for the cookies.
> They were amazing.

Amazing.

I'm sweating.

The phone rings
and I jump,
body airborne
before landing on
my rumpled bed.

It's Victoria.

"Hello?"

"Are you going to help me
pick my outfit, or what?"

I can't speak.

"Danna..."

I read the message again
and again and again
until it makes me dizzy.

"Danna!
What's wrong?"

"He sent me a DM."

Victoria gasps.
"No!"

"Yes!"

"Well, what are you going to say?"

I feel dizzy again,
like the whole world
is tilting,
and I can't tell
if it's leaning more
in my favor
or if it's actually falling,
close to crushing me
completely.

"Danna,
if he didn't like you
he wouldn't be stalking you
on Instagram."

"He said he liked the cookies."
I roll onto my back,
doubt like a giant
resting on my chest.
"What if that's *all* he likes?"

"Well," Victoria says,
"there's only one way
to find out."

I take a deep breath.

"You're brave, Danna."

I exhale.

"You're *brave*, Danna."

I brush the screen,
begin to type.

Hey.

Sweet Tooth

Glad you liked the cookies.
They're an old
family recipe.

                                        Impressive.
                                I can't make anything
                                        from scratch.

Not even cereal?

                                That milk to cornflakes
                                        ratio is tough.
                                Probably why I skip
                                        breakfast.

But it's the most
important meal of the day.
Well,
after dessert.

                                        Sweet tooth?

The biggest.
I've got a blackberry
cheesecake cooling
in the fridge as we speak.

                                        drooling
                        And the special occasion?

Don't need one.
That's what my grandpa
always says about
dessert,
food,

anything that makes
you feel good.

That's actually who it's for.

I thought if I could
recreate
some of his favorite meals
it might help him
remember.

                    Sort of like the music therapy.

Yeah.
Sort of.

                              Has it worked?

Twice.

                              But you keep trying.

I know
it's probably pointless.
Stupid.

                                        No.
                              If it were me
                        I would keep trying
                                       too.

Big and Small and Scary

We talk until
3:00 AM

until my eyes
are burning

and my cell phone
is almost dead.

We talk in memes
and playlists
and puppy videos.

Laughing in
ALL CAPS
while I wheeze
under the blankets
so Mami and Papi
don't hear.

We talk about
Raúl's uncle's
other patients;
the songs they request
over and over;
how Raúl's uncle's
voice cracks
every time he goes for
the high note
in "Hallelujah."

We talk about
Mami's paintings
and Aurora's recipe cards
and the fingerprints
Grandpa left
in every corner
of the world.

We talk about Raúl's mom.
How she isn't sleeping.
How she's still so far away.

We talk about
fried ice cream
and The Mars Volta
and the terrifying possibility
of being abducted by aliens.

We talk about
chemistry
and
driving tests
and
the biggest lie
we've ever told.

We talk
and talk
and talk

about everything

big
and
small
and
scary

until my eyes
are fluttering closed

until my body is
fighting for sleep

until all the things that scared me
six hours ago
don't feel so scary anymore.

Falling

The phone falls
from my grasp
but the rest of me
is still fighting gravity;
so high up,
I'm practically flying.

Maybe falling and flying
are actually the same thing.

Maybe the only difference
is how it makes you feel.

Weightless.
Or
Scared out of your mind.

Fragile.
Or
Free.

I scroll back through
Raúl's messages
and the smile
cutting into my cheeks
actually hurts.

Because I'm
flying
and
falling
at the same time,
headfirst
into something
that feels so good
it just might kill me.

Wings

We douse the walls in white,
sunlight and shadow carving
out ghosts
that watch us work.

I try not to stomp around too much,
in case Grandpa forgets
again
and thinks we really are ghosts
up here.

He and Uncle Moises are in the living
room, watching old Westerns
while Mami and Aunt Veronica run errands.

While Papi and I hang lace curtains
that throw speckles of sunlight
on the newly stained floor.

While we nestle succulent plants
in the windowsill,
and set up Mami's easel,
her new paints in a neat row.

While we cover an old chair
in one of my grandmother's shawls
and roll out a soft shag rug.

It smells like plastic.

Like pretend.

We add another coat of paint,
until every dent, and ding, and stray mark
is buried.

Until everything is a blank canvas.

Except for us.

Then we clean up in silence,
bandannas over our noses and mouths
so we don't choke on the fumes.

Sometimes they're so strong,
Papi's eyes well up
and I wonder if he regrets
constructing this cocoon,
this place where she is supposed to grow
wings.

Because what good are wings
if you can't fly away?

Treasure

"What are you going to do with all these?"

Boxes, still taped shut,
line one of the walls.

More ghosts.

Papi kneels,
examining them up close.

Then he opens one
and it's full of old notebooks,
some leather-bound,
some pocket-size,
some completely falling apart.

"Look at these."
Papi hands me one
and it falls open in my hands
like a yawn,
like something that's been sleeping.

I cradle it, tracing the pages.

The handwriting is messy,
cursive slanted
and falling off
into the margins
like the person who wrote them
was thinking too fast.

Like they were excited.

Like they had to get the words out before...

"Look at the initials."

Papi taps the spine
and I gently turn it over.

M. V.

Marcelino Villarreal.

"These were your grandpa's."
Papi smiles,
pulling out notebook
after notebook.

We sit on the floor,
flipping through pages.

Some are torn,
others stained.

There are drawings of herbs,
of pastries, of pasta.

There are recipes,
measurements listed in number ranges.
Guesses
like he was trying to crack a secret code.

There are descriptions
of dishes I've never even heard of,
descriptions
that make me salivate,
that make my heart race.

There are love letters to chefs
of restaurants in faraway places.

There are old menus clipped
to blank pages;
photographs slid into creases.

There are memories.

There are mysteries.

There are poems.

Answers
to questions
I didn't know to ask,
that I didn't know I craved,
or needed.

"All this time," Papi says.
"They were up here
all this time."

Of course they were,
I think.

Because where there are
dragons
there is always
treasure.

Raúl

Si Dios Quiere

Every time my phone buzzes
my heart turns to glass,
splintered when I see
another dumb text from Manny
or spam for male enhancement pills.

Or a voicemail from Mom
who calls me every day at lunch
to pray over me
before I eat.

Si Dios quiere
Si Dios quiere

"He set me free
for a reason, Raúl."
She melts into the phone.
"We must serve Him
in everything we do."

"I know, Mom."

She hears the annoyance in my voice
and says,
"No, Raúl.
But you will."

And the words strike fear in me
because my life is only
starting.

I am only beginning
to feel safe,

to ask questions,
to think about reaching
for things I might want.

I am finally letting myself *want*.

Pero

si Dios quiere

he can take it away.

To teach me a lesson.
To make me loyal.
To bring me to my salvation.

He can take it all away.

Green

After I finally get off the phone with Mom,
I'm still clutching it
like it might explode.

Like there is something
dangerous inside
ticking down,
ready to detonate
if one more minute passes
without Danna's photo
popping up on my screen.

I shouldn't have said good night.
I shouldn't have fallen asleep.

I should have said something
more.

I go to her Instagram
and scroll,
seven new photos
of Danna covered in paint,
of Danna making pancakes,
of Danna eating salsa verde,
of Danna and a girl who looks a little like her laughing together.

My phone buzzes
and I almost drop it.

Almost.

But then I see her tiny photo,
the notification popping up
like a wink.

I open her message:

So I just realized
that I don't know
your favorite color,
Raúl.

I take a beat,
heart pounding,
and I go back to her Instagram.

I open the photo of her
leaning over her father,
balancing a tortilla chip
topped with salsa verde
as she brings it to her lips,
lime green stuck to her lip gloss
her smile wide and silly and free.

Green,
I type back,
still staring at the salsa verde
stuck to the corner of her mouth,

My favorite color is green.

Bad Influence

I'm in lunch detention.

> And they didn't
> confiscate your phone?

They did.
But then the teacher
fell asleep
and I
confiscated it back.

> You're not worried
> about getting caught?

Coach Reed
never wakes up
until the bell rings.

> Sounds like
> you've had lunch detention
> more than once.

Maybe
a
few
times.

> Are you
> going to be
> a bad influence
> on me?

Only if you
want me
to be.

I'm surprised
a teacher hasn't tried
to take your phone too.

Lunchtime.
I eat outside
so I can play
my guitar.

Dedicated

More like
bored.

How did you
learn to play?

It was mostly
by accident.

The best things
usually are.

I was eight.
Mom took me
to the flea market
for new school clothes.

I saw this booth
of what I thought
were tiny guitars.
Ukuleles.

How hard
did you beg?

There may
have been
tears.

Did they work?

                              The only time.

And a star
was born?

                                   Not quite.

I think you mean
not yet.

Panties

Suddenly, my phone
is vibrating in my hand,
Danna's photo
popping up
like a mirage.

"H-hello?"

Danna's face is
so close to the screen
I can see the freckles
like tiny paw prints
on her nose.

Tracking toward the cliff's edge
of her cheekbones
where dimples crater
like tiny springs.

Her face
is a wilderness
and it doesn't take long
for me to get lost.

"Sorry," she whispers.
"I just wanted...
well...I thought...
maybe I could
listen to you play?"

I'm a tomato again,
her stare a steam turning me to sauce.

"Really?" I say,
a puddle.

Like we're not on a digital island
in a sea of ones and zeroes
but in an empty, dimly lit bar
standing in front of the jukebox,
me flipping the deck to find the
perfect song.

The one that will
have her
reaching for me,
bodies swaying
under a golden
spotlight.

Danna smiles. "Unless
you already have
an audience…"

I flip the screen,
showing her
how alone
I am.

"Really?
No girls tossing you
their panties
while you
serenade them
with sweet love songs?"

"Guess
I'm not
their type."

"Their loss."
She bites her lip.
"Well,
do you need me
to count you in?"

I nod
nervous.

"One,"
she whispers.

I grip the neck of the guitar.

"Two."

I squeeze.

"Three."

I pluck the first string,
not looking at her.

I play
with eyes closed
the song I wrote
for Mom.

The song I wrote for me.

The vela
that I only light
when I'm alone
in my room,
begging for dreams
that don't bite or burn or bleed,
hoping for a nudge
from the Universe,
for a wink from God,
for a promise that can't be broken.

I strum
and pick
and prune the leaves
of my soul.

While Danna watches.
While she listens.

I play
like our island is real
like every note is a silent flare
even though
I'm not sure if
I want to be saved.

Like I'm sending that vela into orbit.
As close to God as I can get.

Finally,

my hands fall off the strings,
the song finished

and I wait for her to blow it out.

My prayer
that still doesn't feel
like it was actually answered.

But when I finally look up
it's Danna
who's been snuffed out,
the screen black.

I hold my guitar
wishing it could hold me back.

My phone dings.

He woke up!
And then the ogre
took my phone.
Bell just rang
so I snatched

it back.

I'm so sorry.

                            It's okay.

I was listening
I swear.

And it was amazing.

And I loved it.

And...
My panties
aren't exciting
or anything
but I would
gladly throw them
at you.

                            I picture
               every non-exciting
                stitch and seam

             until I'm Bolognese,
             until I'm spaghetti,
until I'm a bowl of tomato soup
         a cure for this heart
                     disease
            I wish I'd caught
            a long time ago.

Danna

Raúl Likes

The color green.
Tortillas with butter.
Sweet tea.
Empty movie theaters.
Full moons.
The smell of crackling on the stove.
Grilling.
Eating.
Playing the guitar.
And I think...
I hope...
Raúl likes *me*.

Raúl Hates

Grape jelly.
Mowing the church lawn.
Hailstorms.
Holidays that require hugs.
Justin Bieber.
Fishing.
And most importantly
the fact that his mom
still feels like a stranger,
that she's changed and so has he,
and that there's nothing he can do about it.

Raúl

Danna Likes

The color coral.
S'mores with sea salt.
Mexican hot chocolate.
Birthdays that aren't her own.
Lamplight and electric blankets.
Baking.
Eating.
Laughing.
And I think...
I hope...
Danna likes *me*.

Danna Hates

Mayonnaise.
Running.
Texas in July.
Holidays that don't involve food.
Rachael Ray.
Skiing.
And most importantly
the fact that her grandfather
isn't getting better,
that he'll never get better,
and that there's nothing she can do about it.

Danna

I Knew It

She refuses to wear a blindfold
and is barcly willing to keep
her eyes closed.

So Papi does it for her,
resting his hands over
her eyes while he counts
to three.

"Uno…"

She sighs, impatient.

"Dos…"

I hold my breath.

"Tres."

She blinks
and then she looks,
taking it all in—the white
walls and shelves filled with
brushes and paint. Her easels.

I wait to see what she'll
touch first

but she doesn't move.

Until she clenches her fists,
face twisting

like she might scream
and then she places a hand
over her mouth
and begins to sob.

I lock eyes with Papi.
He bites his lip.
Shakes his head.

Because she hates it.

She hates it.

And I knew she would.

When Papi was dreaming and planning and hoping...
I knew better.

I knew it.

An Introduction

I read the pages with my hands first,
feeling the past like
tiny mountain ranges.
Summits for me to climb
so I can look out on the same terrain,
seeing the world
from the same vantage point
he did.

From a dimly lit booth
in the back of an Italian restaurant
famous
for its apple and sage gnocchi.

On the wooden steps outside
a shipping container-
turned-food truck
where every bánh mì sandwich is topped
with a sunny-side up egg.

A portrait of
an appetite—
even older than I am—
for secret sauces and prime cuts of meat and
peppers crossbred to blow your top off.

For adventure and romance and a satisfaction
you can taste.

Grandpa chased down
lampreys in France
and oysters in Japan
and vintage wine in Spain.

He tasted percebes in Portugal
casu marzu in Sardinia
blood sausage in Argentina.

And as I read his words—
scribbled
in Spanish and English
and sometimes other languages too—
I am alive in those places.

Like they're just on the other side
of my bedroom door.

Like if I twist the knob and
push it open, there I'll be
standing on a rocky coastline
with a waffle cone full of rose petal ice cream,
or in a treetop cafe overlooking the Guadalupe River
with a plate of chicken-fried steak bigger than my face.

I see him there too,
cutting it up with the owner,
greeting the line cooks and head chefs,
making everyone laugh
like they know him,
before he saves it all in his notebook—
every bite, every word, every name of a stranger
who he made feel special.

His notebooks laid open on my bed,
in my lap,
on my knees,
I feel special too.

Because here it is:
Everything he's lost.
Everything we've been trying to get back.

The key to his memories.
To the parts of him I never knew.

A reminder.

An introduction.

A miracle.

Clues

Victoria sits on the floor,
on the only square foot of carpet
not covered in journals
and scraps of paper.

I've even started covering the walls
with writing of my own.
The lists that are my
answer to everything.

Checkboxes and tick marks and line after line
like I'm fishing
for hope.

"I can't believe he went to all these places,"
Victoria says, gripping the pages,
salivating over them the same way I have been.

"Careful," I tell her, taking the notebook
she's holding and smoothing out the pages.

She turns to the other stacks,
organized by region and then date.

I starred the cities and countries he seemed to love the most,
trips every few years to the same
East African beaches and South American rainforests
and European castles.

I cross-referenced them with his favorite dishes.
The foods he had to taste in every language,
on every strip of land,
to see the way it evolved and expanded
and became something new.

Cheesecake
French Fries
Chicken Noodle Soup

Ice Cream
Roasted Pork
Fresh Baked Bread

It took me six hours.
I hardly slept.

"So what's your plan?"
Victoria stands in front of my notes
tacked to the wall,
her hands on her hips
like she's waiting
for her marching orders.

"Plan?"

"That's what this is," she says,
"isn't it?"

I stand next to her,
the words rearranging themselves
until they're not just lists,
not just clues.

They're a map.

A map of Grandpa's memories.

Of his heart.

"The plan is to find a place that serves each dish
or to recreate them ourselves."

Victoria looks at me. "The plan is to feed him..."

And I know that it won't be that simple,
that after every step forward
will be two steps back.
But in those brief moments
when he's awake and aware and
almost himself again,
I can see in his eyes
the hunger for
something.

So, "Yes," I tell her, "the plan is to feed him."

He's Here

This time when the doorbell rings
I scream.

Because I'm still in my pajamas
with my hair a mess.

Because I forgot Raúl and his uncle
would be here at noon.

"What the hell, Danna?"
Victoria shakes me.

I grab her face.
"I need you to preheat the oven."

Her nose wrinkles,
confused.

"375 degrees."

She cocks her head.

"He's here."

Then her eyes widen.
"He's here?"

This time we both scream.

The Girl in the Mirror

I tear through the clothes in my closet,
wire hangers squealing.

There's the section of tank tops
I never wear
because I hate the way
my arms look.

There's the summer blouses
in the citrus shades I love—yellow, orange, red—
but that Mami says make me look too dark.

Touching the fabric
summons her voice.

Silk is too unforgiving.
Crop tops show your stretch marks.
V-necks make your boobs look too big.

Dressing room meltdowns
and
Family photo fiascos
and
Pre-party disasters
play behind my eyes
until they burn with tears.

Arguing over this body that
won't fit
into the keyhole
that unlocks
my mother's love.

"The blue one." Victoria's voice is by my ear.
"White jeans and your gold hoops.
It's perfect."

Perfect.

She says it like it's nothing.
Like it's easy.
As easy as being me.

I don't believe her until I get dressed
and catch my reflection in the mirror.

I look tired
but the race to get ready
has painted me pink
and my hair looks cute
tied back in a high pony.
The blue top makes my eyes sparkle
and the white jeans
hug me
in all the right places.

I don't look like
Victoria
or
one of Mami's
paintings.

I look like me.

Suddenly, the girl in the mirror smiles
and I smile back.

Labios

The chamucos are still cooling
on the kitchen counter,
the smell snaking through the house,
leading people by the mouth
to my masterpiece.

Raúl's uncle tosses one
from palm to palm,
impatient. Needing
the sweet pastry
in his mouth
even if it burns.

Papi examines his with
pinched lips, measuring
the circumference of each circle.

Victoria stabs her ring finger
in the center,
before scooping out the cream cheese
and licking her finger clean.

Grandpa takes his in both hands
before taking a giant bite.

Raúl is the only one who waits,
watching the way the sugar sparkles,
throwing glances in my direction,
like he is bracing
for something
mind-blowing.

We lock eyes
across the kitchen island
and take a bite
at the same time,

his face becoming
an entire universe.

The sugar,
like more stardust,
presses
to his nose.
The cream cheese filling
sticks to his lips,
his tongue
tracing across them
while he blushes.

And my brain switches
to Spanish,
to Papi's love language
and maybe mine too.

And for the rest of the day
all I can think about
es azúcar
y labios
y besando bajo las estrellas.

Raúl

On the Tip of My Tongue

Every time I saw her
flitting back and forth across the kitchen,
my uncle's voice in my ear,
singing about love,
I wanted to say
something.

When we stood around
the kitchen island,
waiting for the pastries
to cool,
that need to speak
finally
became a solid thing.

Words in the shape of
hope.

Do you want to go out with me?
my eyes said.

Do *you* want to go out with *me*?

The words poured from me
in the sweat
sticking the collar of my shirt
to the back of my neck.

Do you want to *go out* with me?

As sweet
as the sugar
on the tip of my tongue.

But I couldn't say the words
aloud.

Couldn't take the risk.

Couldn't do anything
but chew on them
with the chamuco
like butter,
like heaven,
that tasted
like the answer
to all my questions.

Old School

Hey.

Hey.

So my mom says
you're going to give
my uncle diabetes.

Was that before
or after
she took
a bite
herself?

After.

Maybe I'll
try my hand
at something
sugar-free.

Blasphemy.

For your mom,
I am willing
to go
to the dark side.

What's her favorite dessert?

. . .

Whenever she had a bad day
she'd take me to Dairy Queen
for banana splits.

Old school.

I don't even like bananas.
But they're not so bad
when they're covered
in vanilla ice cream.

Everything's better
when it's covered
in vanilla ice cream.

True.

Yeah.

So.

So?

I was thinking...

Yeah?

And I was hoping...

???

And I was wondering...

Do you want to go out with me?

How dare you beat me to it!

It's Not a Hymn

Each note is a shallow prick,
tattooing me with the memory
of my courtyard concert.

I play the song
over and over and over again
until the island starts to feel real
until I start to believe that it could be.

"Which hymn is that?"
Mom's in the doorway.

It swallows her,
a hungry mouth.

Like every time I see her
I'm waiting for her to disappear.

To vanish in a thunderclap.
To disintegrate in a thick fog.

I answer her, just to prove that she's real.

"It's not a hymn," I say.
"I wrote it."

I think she'll tell me that it's beautiful.
I think she'll ask me to play it again.

But instead
she stiffens
as if she can suddenly sense the mouth;
the danger she's in.

She *looks* at me like we're in *danger*...

and then she says,
"Have you finished your homework?"

My chemistry book lies on the bed.
Another open mouth.
She wags a finger at it.

"No more music until you finish your homework."

Bad Dreams

The sound of her
twisted up
in the blankets,
groaning
against
invisible binds,
wrenches me from
my sleep.

If you could even call it that.
Teeth grinding.
Chest covered in sweat.
While I pretend not to see the time
glowing red
on my nightstand.

Breathing with my eyes closed
and my mind wide open.

Not quite here.
Not quite there.

Clutching myself till morning.

Until her bad dreams woke me first.

Like I was dreaming them too.

I ease out into the hallway
and make my way
to her door.

It's slightly ajar
and I barely press against it,
opening it just
an inch more.

So I can see her face.
Gripped in fear.
Like this feeling in my chest.
Knowing that even if I touched her,
if I brought her a glass of water
like she used to when
I was scared of
monsters
under my bed,
there is no waking up from this.

No opening her eyes
and realizing it was all pretend.

So instead
I just watch her breathe
and wrestle with
things I can't see.

Things that can't see me.
That don't care that I'm her son.
That it's 2:00 AM.
That she's supposed to be free.

That I'm tired.

That I'm *so fucking* tired.

That she is too.

Empty

Shakespeare's *Othello* plays
on the giant screen
at the front of the room.

At first, I sit up straight
forcing my eyes to focus,
begging
my mind to stop circling
sleep.

I'm exhausted.
And even though I hate school
my body feels lighter here,
taking the darkness of the room,
the low murmur from the speakers,
the still bodies breathing and quiet
as a sign
that I am safe.

That it's okay for my muscles to relax.
That it's okay to fold my arms on my desk,
to rest my head on my wadded-up hoodie.

To close my eyes
and sleep.

The drowsiness spreads.
My muscles relent.
And with every deep breath
I feel like a fuel gauge,
the indicator slowly moving away from the letter E.

From empty.

Until Ms. Choi
jostles me

awake,
hisses for me to
sit up straight.

Even though my head is pounding and my eyes burn
and I can't remember the last time I slept through the
night.

Nothing is more important than Shakespeare.

Crisis

My hoodie is covered in drool
by the time I get to next period.
My body stealing every second,
every micro-nap interrupted
by a rough hand on my shoulder,
an angry voice by my ear.

And I want to cry,
to beg for one more minute
of the rest I can't find at home.

Because she's there and she's broken and I don't know how
to fix it.

But no one asks me why I can't keep my eyes open,
if I'm sick and need to see the nurse,
if they should call my uncle,
if I need to go home.

It doesn't matter what I need.

So I clench my fists
under my desk
and pretend to pay attention
to Mr. Duggan
as he drones on about the
Cold War
and the Cuban Missile
Crisis.

While I pretend that word doesn't
stoke something in me.

Crisis.
Crisis.

A tiny flare in the back of my mind
in the back of my throat
burning
like my entire world is on fire
and nobody cares but me.

The Sweetness Underneath

By eighth period
I'm hanging
on by a thread.

But Mr. Rodriguez
sees.

I know he sees
because in the middle of his lecture
on kinetic molecular theory
he casually walks over to his desk,
grabs a jar of peppermints,
and starts handing them out
to the entire class.

And I remember how he said
before the midterm
that peppermints can help
with increasing memory,
lowering stress,
and fighting fatigue.

I place the candy on my tongue
and let it burn,
the tiny sparks
travelling to the inside of my nose
up my spinal cord
and straight to my brain.

And there was no jerking my body back to the
present.
No scowling.
No making me feel like shit.

The mint finally dissipates and all I'm left with
is the sweetness underneath. And I wish
it would last forever.

I wish all sorts of things did.

Like those banana splits
Mom and I shared in the parking lot
at Dairy Queen
when everything bad
in the world was instantly better
with a little sugar on top.

F Is for Fucked

Just before the bell rings
Mr. Rodriguez passes out the
unit test
we took last week.

Facedown
like he always does
because the numbers
mean more
to some kids than others.

I haven't decided yet
if they mean anything to me.

Not like they do to Mom,
who needs to measure me
in letters and percentages
because unlike men,
they don't lie.

And that's what I'm becoming.
A man who will either take from the world
or give something back.

"Don't embarrass me, mijo."

She says it all the time.
Like it's in my nature.
Like embarrassing her is the default
and being good
means being someone else.

The boy who gets straight As,
who is eager to please,
who is college-bound
just because his mother says so.

But she's not sitting with me in this desk,
holding the pencil as I bubble in answers
on a test that feels like a trap.

She's not showing up to school tired
trying to take notes,
to pay attention,
to smile every once in a while
so my teachers will have mercy on me.

She's not here holding my hand.
No one is.

Mr. Rodriguez slides the paper in front of me
and I wait for him to walk away
before I fold back the corner
and peek at my grade
on a test I barcly remember taking
because I blinked and suddenly
the bell was ringing
and I'd only answered question one.

As soon as I check the grade,
I wish I hadn't.

"Don't embarrass me, mijo."

Because that's exactly what an F will do.

F for Failure.
F for Fucked.

And I try to feel sorry.
I really do.

But all I feel is the indicator
falling
falling
back
to
empty.

Sleep

Mom isn't home yet.
She's still at the church,
hired by my uncle to help with childcare
because there was
no application
no
Check here
if you've ever been convicted of a
felony.

I lie on the couch
thinking about her
on her knees,
helping them color
and write their names.

Helping them hold the crayon, the pencil,
their hand
so small in hers.
Like mine used to be.

Before I understood the words,
"Don't embarrass me, mijo,"
because she never thought to say them.

Because I was tiny and perfect and always made her
laugh.

I stare at the popcorn ceiling until
the dots begin to quiver, slowly
moving into the shape of us.

One body holding us both.

Then me in her arms
while she sways
and tries to rock me to sleep.

Her hair a mess.
Her eyes as red as mine.

Please. Please. Please.

She chanted the words,
too tired to sing,
because I was clingy and colicky and she was only
seventeen.

Just a year older than I am now.

A baby, Uncle Mario always says
when he talks about the day she told
their parents she was pregnant.

Your mom was just a baby.

And captain of the drill team.
Student council treasurer.
Future robotics major.

She was pretty and popular and she gave it all up
so she could be awake with me instead,
lying on her side next to my crib,
crying in the middle of the night.

And now it's my turn.
To make tough choices.
To lie awake and worry.

To carry this burden the way she carried me.

Danna

Shape

I'm thumbing through the hangers in my closet when she sits
    on my bed.

"Can we talk?"

She's staring at her hands in her lap and I think it's about the
    attic.
How she didn't say a word about all the work we'd done.
How, after a few minutes of crying into her hands,
she asked us to leave her alone.

"Sure."

I make my way over and sit next to her.
My knee rubs against her leg and I scoot over an inch.

"I heard you've got a date tonight."

My stomach drops.
Because she's not here to explain or apologize or even say
    thank you.
She's here to…to…

"Danna, I just want to make sure that no matter how things
    turn out,
you're going to be okay."

"What do you mean, 'no matter how things turn out'?"

"Your father says Raúl is a nice boy."

"He is."

"But sometimes boys act one way in front of parents
and then become someone completely different when you're
alone with them."

"Raúl's not like that."

"But he could be. And..." She straightens. "I just don't want
        you
to get your hopes up. You hit puberty at such a young age.
Boys have been looking at you a certain way since you were
        ten years old.
Grown men too."

"Wait. You think Raúl only asked me out because of the way
        I look?"

"Because of your shape, Danna."

Your shape.

"Maybe I can help you pick out an outfit that's a little bit
        more modest.
Something you'll feel comfortable in."

Comfortable.
Comfortable?

Suddenly, I feel every inch of my body
like none of it is *real* or *mine* or *safe.*

But not because some grown man is whistling at me
from across the street or a guy at school is trying to
slip his cell phone between my legs to snap a picture.

Those things hurt.
They scare me.

But this...

Mami and her warning.
Mami and her words.

The ones she said and the ones she didn't.

Your shape is dangerous.

Your shape is your fault.

Your *shape* is *dangerous.*

Your *shape* is your *fault.*

"Please leave."
I can't think,
my body speaking for me.

"Danna."

"You told us to leave you alone," I say, remembering
the attic. "Now I'm asking to be alone too."

She's Wrong

"That woman! Danna, she's...
she's...she's wrong, okay?
She's a liar and a monster
and you're beautiful and...
Jesus! Why does she always
fucking do this? There's
something wrong with her,
Danna. Not you. It's never
been you. And you're not the
only one with those sucios
ogling you without permission.

"It's not because of your shape, Danna,
it's because of your fucking gender.

"And she knows that. That's what
drives me fucking nuts is that
she knows she's putting the
blame where it doesn't belong.
It's not about what you wear
or what you weigh. It's about
men! It's about this world!
And the fact that she would
take that truth, that is so ugly
and scary and painful, and
make you feel like it's
something you did or
someone you are. I hate
her for doing that to you.
Did you hear me, Danna?
She's wrong!"

I Hear You

I hold the phone away from my ear,
waiting for Victoria to yell again.

"Danna?"

I wipe the tears from my eyes,
and let out a breathy laugh.

Because she's right.
Because I love her.

"Yeah, Victoria,
I hear you."

Raúl

Shit

My phone buzzes from the arm
of the couch before sliding
down and landing with a thud
against my head.

Shit.

It felt like I was asleep for only seconds.
A single blink.

But my alarm is screaming that it's half past six.

Shit. Shit. Shit.

There's a text from Danna
about looking forward to seeing me
and another
fifteen minutes later.

An ellipses.

And I wonder what's at the end
of it. Anger.
Rejection. A door
slamming in my face.

My stomach sinks
and I think about pretending
to be sick,
about lying.

But that's what we do at home.
Pretending that everything's fine.

That because Mom's finally home,
everything's fixed.

I don't want to lie to Danna.

So I race around the house,
brushing my teeth,
running wet fingers through my hair.
Splashing water on my face.

I slap myself a few times too.
Wake up. Wake up. Wake up.

And then I bolt, unchaining the bike
I ride to and from the gas station
when I'm desperate for a midnight snack.

I pedal like my life depends on it
and pray I don't smell like ass
by the time I get to her door.

Danna

Stress Baking

After six outfit changes,
a dozen failed attempts
at using Victoria's eyeliner,
three trips to the bathroom
thinking I needed to pee again
even though I just went,
and half a bag of
hot Cheetos,
Raúl still isn't here.

I text him
twice and
still nothing.

I think about calling but I don't.
I think about changing back into my pajamas but I don't.
I think about crying to Victoria over FaceTime but I don't.

Instead, I rummage through the pantry
before grabbing a couple of mixing bowls
and dumping ingredients
into each one.

I make a mess
with my hands,
feeling the textures,
the coolness
on my skin.

I roll the cookie dough between my palms,
lining up the balls in a neat row,
trying not to think about

Raúl
laughing with his asshole friends
about standing me up.

I shove the pan in the oven
and watch the clock,
until the ticking is louder
than my own pulse
throbbing between my ears.

Maybe he changed his mind.
But we've been texting every night.
Maybe he got into a car accident.
But he's riding his bike.
Maybe he got hit by a car and he's dead.

I pinch my eyes shut,
pleading with my brain to stop
making lies.
To stop
making lists.

Maybe there's someone else...
Maybe it was all a joke...
Maybe he thinks I'm fat...
Maybe Mami is right...

Stop. Stop. Stop. Stop!

The oven dings and I jump.

The cookies come out
warm
and brown
and smelling like heaven.

I breathe them in
and my brain finally
goes quiet.

Then I hear the sound of the doorbell
and through the stained glass on the other side
of the door
I see Raúl
pacing and nervous
and my heart lodges in my throat.

Raúl

Bomb

The door is closed
and dark
like no one's home.

Maybe she's not.
Maybe she realized I wasn't coming
and found someone else to take her out.

Or maybe she *is* inside.
Still waiting…

I drop my bike in the front yard,
bound up the porch steps, and take a deep breath.
Then I reach for the doorbell,
press the pad of my finger against it
like it's the detonator on a bomb.

I hear footsteps.
I straighten.
The door eases open.

It's Danna.

"I'm so sorry
I overslept
I didn't mean to
but I haven't been sleeping
and I lay down for like two seconds
and all of a sudden I woke up
and it was almost 6:30
and I rushed to get ready

and I don't know if you even still wanna go out
but—"

She guides something soft and sweet into my mouth.

I taste the bitterness of the dark chocolate chips
dancing with the lightness of the molasses.
A hint of vanilla.
Something even sweeter,
like pudding.
Banana pudding.
And finally, the tartness of the cherries.

"What do you think?" she asks.

I swallow it down,
the flavors still lingering,
my mind transported.

Mom looking over at me
in the passenger seat,
wiping the whipped cream
from my chin and face.

One of a million memories
I've shared with Danna
over text.

A millisecond
of my life
she thought was worth
remembering
too.

"It's delicious," I say.

She smiles. "They're for your mom.
Sugar-free banana split cookies."

Danna

Mena's

Since my cookies are better
than any banana split Raúl
has ever had,
he lets me choose
our destination.

He doesn't know
that in my purse
is a list
of all of the restaurants in Austin
where my grandfather once sat,
mulling over the tastes
and textures
of whatever was on his plate,
the sensations scribbled
on scraps of paper
I'm not even halfway
through reading.

And at the very top
is Mena's,
a teal and white oasis
with pink and orange accents
and picnic tables
that look like rainbows.

I make Raúl pose beneath
the rooster
on the restaurant sign
before snapping a photo.

He crosses his arms,
a line running along his bicep
and I think he might be flexing.

"Cute."
I show him
before we make our way
to the line,
the smell of guajillo
filling my lungs
as warm as the smile
Raúl's face hasn't let go of
since I climbed onto his bike pegs
and rested my hands on his shoulders.

The Cherry on Top

Grandpa used to take
Victoria and me
out to lunch
every Sunday
after church.

For
Chocolate Shakes and Bacon Cheeseburgers
Bolo de Laranja and Piri Piri Chicken Pastries
Basque Burnt Cheesecake and Cochinita Pibil
Pecan Praline Pistolette and Lemon Pepper Catfish
Italian Cream Cake and Pastrami Sandwiches

Dessert always first
because, "You never know
what could happen, mijas."

Sometimes it was an asteroid
striking Earth
or a sudden torrential flood.
An alien invasion.
The zombie
apocalypse.

I would shudder
at the thought
of having my brain eaten
while Victoria would
jump up and pretend to
aim a machine gun.

"Don't worry,"
she'd always say.
"I'll protect you."

Then,
for just a moment,

Grandpa would get
serious and say,
"Promise me."
He'd look us
both in the eyes.
"Promise me you'll
always take care of
each other."

We'd nod our heads.
Promising him.
Promising each other.

And then Victoria
would duck
away from the window
like we'd been spotted.

"Vampires,"
Grandpa would whisper
before waving the waitress
over to order a plate of garlic
while Victoria and I
howled with laughter.

Like every disaster scenario—
the unknown itself—
was just the
splice
of a line,
the thing that made us tingle
and feel more alive.

The cherry on top,
he would say.

Now it's a fly in the soup.
The kind of unexpected surprise that turns your stomach.
Because none of us expected this.

For the disaster to strike
so close
to home,
so close
to his heart.

That's what it feels like we've lost
sometimes...

The part of him that was more alive than the rest.

Always following his sweet tooth
like a compass
that I am clutching so tight,
trying to read,
to follow.

Because he's not the only one who's been forgetting.
All those Sunday lunches.

The jokes that had us spewing orange juice
from our noses.

The stories he painted behind our eyes
better than any movie I'd ever seen.

So when Raúl asks
why I'm ordering dessert first,
I use my grandpa's words,
trying to reignite the spark,
to make the unknown feel
like the cherry on top of the sundae.

Like the *sweetest* bite
of life
Grandpa
believed it
to be.

In My Bones

I don't mean to write a poem.

But when I take that first bite
of the strawberry guava ice cream
Grandpa raved about
in an article for *Bon Appétit* magazine,
the cold hitting my tongue
as the tartness spreads,
I feel a rhythm
in my teeth.

In my bones.

The words showing
up on my skin
in braille;
goosebumps sprouting
in a language that
only knows how to dance.

I take that first bite
and the poem
writes itself.

Begging to be typed
into the Notes app
on my phone
where I keep my lists
that might not actually be
lists
after all.

Strawberry Guava Ice Cream

My cold lips scream pink,
sticky and sweet while he stares
at me like I'm a ripened fruit.

While I stare back
wanting to be plucked
como una uva off the vine.

The perfect shape
for his mouth
that is just as pink as mine.

Right in Front of You

"I'm sorry," he says again,
"I feel like a jerk
for being late."

"It's okay," I tell him
even though my heart
almost shattered
when I thought he'd
stood me up.

"It's just..."
He wraps his hands
around the stem
of the glass bowl
of ice cream,
now empty.

"Yeah...?"
I lean forward,
making my voice soft.

"I've been having trouble sleeping."
He meets my eyes.
"I hear my mom
tossing and turning at night,
having bad dreams..."

"That's probably normal," I offer,
"after all she's been through."

I don't even know the half of it.
Just that Raúl's mom was in prison
for something that wasn't her fault.
That she came back different.
That even though she's home
Raúl still misses her.

I hear it in his voice,
this longing for someone
who isn't supposed to be lost.

And I know exactly how he feels,
trying to find someone who's
right in front of you.

Grandpa.

Mami.

Both of them behind glass.
Miles and miles away.

But Raúl isn't.
He's right here and so am I.

Close enough to touch.
So I do.

I reach across the table
and take his hand in mine,
an apology of my own,
while he tells me about
the person his mother used to be,
the person he used to be too.

You're a Writer

"When I worry," I tell him,
"I like to make lists."

"What kind of lists?"

I pull out the scrap of paper,
my compass,
and slide it across the table.

Every food and drink
I've tried so far,
coffee and chorreadas de piloncillo
still the only
successes.

I pull a pen from my purse
and scribble
strawberry guava ice cream.

"The lists...
they make me feel
more in control.
Sometimes they're plans.
Sometimes they're gut checks.
Reminders that my world
isn't falling apart.
Safety nets to keep
that from happening."

"You're a writer," Raúl says,
"like he was."

My cheeks warm.
"I guess I am."

"And writing things down,
it helps?" he asks,
earnest.

"Sometimes."
I exhale.
"It's harder when it's all in here."
I tap my forehead,
our hands breaking apart
for a second.

And I think he'll
leave the space
between us.

That I was too bold
to have held his hand.

But suddenly, he
finds my fingers again.
"That's how I feel when
I talk to you.
Like everything loud
between my ears
goes quiet."

I smile,
my face as red
as the ice cream
melted at the bottom
of my bowl.

"Me too," I say.
"I like talking to you too."

Midnight Snack

It's only nine o'clock but when I see the light on
in Grandpa's room, I can't help but sneak inside
like he used to do after a late flight,
landing on the edge of my bed with a
a box of fudge from Mackinac Island,
toffee from Jaipur,
dark chocolate from Ecuador.

I'd open my eyes to the sound of him
rustling the package or peeling back the plastic
like he was opening a present without me.

Then he'd break off a piece of something sweet
before pressing a finger to his lips
making me promise not to tell.

We'd eat and talk in hushed whispers,
Grandpa telling me about the people he'd met
and what the insides of their homes looked like.
The animals he'd seen that I was adamant about naming.

Jorge the elephant.
Pamela the ostrich.
Mickey the manatee.

This time I'm the one who's come bearing gifts—
two spoons sticking up from the pint of
strawberry guava ice cream.

He sits up in bed
and at first,
I worry that I've woken him
from a dream.

That I've startled him.
That he's scared.
But then, in the dim light, he smiles.

I lead a spoonful of ice cream to his lips
and he squeezes his eyes shut,
the cold such a shock
that he laughs.

And then, "Did I ever tell you
about the guava I ate in Calvillo?
The fruit is sweeter there.
Something about the family—the Landeros.
They make everything—cookies, pastries, chocolates—
each one named for one of Don Saul's daughters.
Pero the wine... ¡Hijue!
I've never been so drunk in my life."

Raúl

Trigger

I walk my bike up the driveway,
the house phosphorescent,
light pouring from every window
and it reminds me of a prison
yard. Of eyes as bright
as the sun.

Another monster,
breathing fire,
still following her.

As soon as I push
the door open
I feel the heat.

"Where have you been?"

I hear Uncle Mario in the shower.
The clock reads 9:13 PM—almost an hour
before my curfew. But she doesn't
know that.

All she knows
is that it's dark. That I'm wearing
my uncle's cologne.
That my lips are stained red
from the strawberry guava ice cream,
from the way I kept pinching
them between my teeth
because all I wanted to do was kiss her.

But we didn't.

We just talked. Because I like talking to Danna.
Because there's something about her eyes that
coaxes out the words I'm normally
too afraid to say out loud.

Mom doesn't know that either.

"Raúl," she snaps,
"I said where have you been?"

I look down.
"I had a date."

She puts her hands on her hips.
"With who?"

I tell her about Danna.

She remembers.
"The girl with the cookies."

That's when I hand her Danna's latest batch.

She doesn't even look at them.
"Is she the reason
you failed
your chemistry test?"

"What?" I shake my head, confused.
"No."

"Then what's the reason?
Because now that I'm home,
you think you can slack off?
That's not how
I raised you,
Raúl."

243

The words load themselves
into the chamber of my mouth,
bullets I can't bite down on hard enough.

Because she has me walking on eggshells.
Because my grades are all she cares about.
Because she won't stop *pretending*.

But I can't.
I *can't* pretend.

Instead,
I pull the trigger and say,
"You haven't been raising me
at all."

Then I watch the words
lodge themselves
in her gut.

And in the silence
we both
bleed.

Grounded

She takes
my phone
like I'm a child
like it's a toy
like it's not the only life raft I have.

Like living with her in this apartment
isn't as lonely
as a deserted island.

Every text a flare
shot into the night sky.

Now
an SOS to no one.

Prayer

I wait until the house is quiet
and it's late enough for dreams.

For my mother's insomnia
to lose its grip
and sleep to pull her under
where I know the sounds
won't reach.

I pluck the strings
one at a time,
needing to feel
the vibrations
against my skin.

Buzzing
like I'm not alone
in this house,
in this body,
in this moment
when I am missing her the most.

Soon my fingers are searching,
making lists of my own,
of all her favorite songs,
my gut stopping on
"God's Child"
by Selena and David Byrne.

I strum what I remember,
feeling my way through the rest,
splintered memories
that I drag into the present,
that I send up like more flares.

To a God I don't trust
to answer them,
to even hear me when I call.

But maybe *she* can.

Half asleep.
Breathing deep.
Notes snaking down the hall and
slipping beneath her skin.

Come back.
Come back.
Come back.

It Helps

I linger in the doorway
like Mr. Rodriguez's classroom
is made of lava,
the C I need at the center—
treasure or trap,
I'm not entirely sure.

But there's no leveling
up unless I step inside.

"I was hoping you might come by."
Mr. Rodriguez cleans his glasses,
motions for me to have a seat.

But he doesn't reach for the Expo marker
or for the test I flatten on the desk.
He just watches me,
like he's looking for cracks.

"You look tired," he finally says.

I scrape a hand down my face,
wishing it knew how to lie.

"Something keeping you up?"

My mouth fixes itself
to do what the rest of my body can't.
"My fault.
Video games."

"Not the best idea on a school night."
He clasps his hands, leans in.
"But I'm happy to hear it's nothing serious."

I keep my eyes down. "Nope."

"I have trouble sleeping sometimes,"
he goes on. "Just got a lot going on up here."
He taps his forehead. "Home stuff.
Work stuff. The million things on my to-do list."
He meets my eyes. "So I started taking long
walks in the evening. Gets the blood pumping.
Helps me clear my head. I come home and
sink straight into bed."

"And it...helps?"
I forget my armor again.
The words fall out.

Mr. Rodriguez smiles.
"It helps."

Do-over

We work through each problem
one at a time.

Retracing my missteps.

And it's so easy
to scrub away
the mistakes.

To try again.

I wish real life was like that.
That there were do-overs
and second chances.

Maybe that's why Mom's
being so hard on me.
Because she *knows*.

Life isn't a test you can take again.

You either pass or you fail
and the older I get,
the less time she has to
stack the deck in my favor,
to have any say in
who I'll end up being.

Start Again

Behind my eyes there's a blue light
and blinking cursor,
as I imagine
how to explain
to Danna why I didn't
call or text or
ask her on a
second date.

I arrange and rearrange the words,
delete
and start again.

Until the time on the clock
is almost midnight.
Another day wasted
on worrying about
all the things
I can't control.

But then the clock
blinks
12:00 AM. And it's like
the eraser end of a pencil.

The do-over
I desperately needed.

And suddenly I'm throwing
on a shirt and
reaching
for my sneakers,
holding my breath
as I slip
into the hallway.

The Next Terrible Thing

There's a light
on in the bathroom
and as I ease closer
I hear the water running,
and slapping the tiles,
pipes whistling from the
pressure.

And then I hear
her breathing.

Soft and then hard.

The sound muffled
like she's biting
her own fist.

Sobs
like she wants
to scream.
Like she can't
catch her breath.

I hear my mother crying behind the closed bathroom door
and my knees quake, trying to force me to the ground.

Because it hurts
so much
to hear it.

Memories turned to sound,
the past so painful
it makes her shudder.

I shake too.

And then I taste her tears,
streaming from my eyes,
pouring into my own mouth.

Until I can't take it.

Thinking about what they did to her.

When she was alone
and scared and waiting
for the next terrible thing.

I press my hand to the door,
so soft I know she can't hear it.

I lean in and *listen*,
gritting my teeth,
the lump in my throat
like fire.

Because I can hear it in the way she weeps.
She is still waiting for the next terrible thing.

Danna

Just Another Monster

I followed the recipe
to a tee,
the stew swirling and red
like the inside of a volcano.

The perfect balance
of salt and heat
with a roux that
almost made Papi weep.

Another poem
I couldn't wait
to feed Grandpa.

"Your brother's secret recipe,"
I said. "Remember?"

But today
he didn't.

He didn't remember.

Tío Héctor
or their yearly trip to New Orleans.

The okra
their mother used to grow
under a blazing south Texas sun.

The smell of caldo
simmering for hours
on Sundays after church.

But worst of all
he didn't remember
that he's safe with me.
That I'm his flesh and blood.
That feeding each other is what we do.

Instead,
he knocked the spoon
out of my hand,
recoiling
like I was just
another monster.

Revenge

"He still hasn't texted you back?"
Victoria lies on my bed,
feet in my lap
while I paint
tiny white daisies
on her toenails.

I shake my head
and try not to cry.
Not yet.
Not over a boy I barely know
who ghosted me after our first date.

Victoria sits up on her elbows,
eyeing me. "Forget him.
He's an asshole
and so not worth your time."

As soon as she says the word
asshole, I get a pang
in my stomach.
Because I should have known.
I should have seen it coming.
But I didn't.

"I feel like an idiot."

"Cállate. Don't go there, Danna.
Getting ghosted—it happens
to all of us."

I groan.
Because that's not true.
Things like this
don't happen to Victoria.
And even if they did,

there would be a line of drooling
suitors, waiting for their turn.

Like she's a prize to be won.

But I'm not even a consolation.

Victoria snaps her fingers.
"Get out of your head."

I fall back
onto a pile of pillows.
"How?"

Victoria looks from the window
back to my face.
"By getting out of this house."

Lengua

The room is full of strangers,
barely dressed
and tipping back shot glasses
while Bad Bunny's baritone voice
slides smooth from the mouths
of busted speakers.

No wire cage to muffle the sound,
the cone throbbing
like I'm staring at the
center of my own eardrum.

I tug on the body-con dress
Victoria let me borrow,
shrugging my denim jacket close,
trying not to think
to wonder
if *this* is why.

Why Raúl didn't call.
Why he didn't text.

If he disappeared
because my body
made a promise
the rest of me
couldn't keep.

I didn't even kiss him
good night.

Or maybe
he wouldn't
have wanted me to.

Maybe
up close

he finally saw
what Mami does.

That I don't fit.

Stop.
Stop.
Stop.

Someone walks by
with shot glasses
and I reach for one,
tossing it back.

I choke on cheap tequila
but as soon as the burn
begins to dull
I'm reaching for another.

Until I'm not thinking about
Mami
or
Raúl.

Until I'm not thinking
about anything.

"Dance with me."
Victoria takes my hand,
spinning me in circles.

I sidestep between bodies,
pushed from one partner to the next.

I dance with a guy in a black
flat-billed snapback.

I grind on a girl in a tight red dress
and a bright orange bucket hat.

I list the other outfits and accessories:
a bright pink one-shoulder crop top
and

gold bamboo earrings
and
baby blue Jordans
and
loose-laced Timbs
on bodies that I count
like sheep jumping
over an electric fence,
music shocking them to life
even though the purple strobe lights
make me feel like I'm in a dream.

Wake up,
someone whispers.

I take another shot instead.

Then I stumble
into someone's arms
or maybe I'm sitting
on their lap.

But suddenly I can feel their
whole body
on my body.

And the music is so loud.
And my head is swimming.

And then their tongue is in my mouth.

Fat and slimy
and chasing
the air from my lungs.

I gag
and then spit.
"¡Saca tu lengua de mi boca!"

But the guy just laughs.
Still holding my hips.
Gripping me hard.

Not letting go
until I fall forward
and hurl
all over his jeans.

Joy Like…

Victoria's makeup
drips down her face
from laughing
and screaming
and running
as fast as we can.

"You…"
she gasps,
"you…"
She clutches herself.
"I can't believe you did that!"

I cross my legs,
almost tripping
over a parking block.
"I'm going to pee my pants!"

Victoria snorts,
both of us wheezing
and barely able to take a breath.

"Stop it…stop it…"
I plead, tears streaming
down my face.

My grin is so wide it hurts.
Victoria waves a hand,
trying to compose herself.

But we're a mess.
A wild, blubbering mess
eliciting car honks
and angry yells
for us to get out of the way.

But I don't know the way.
Because I'm drunk.
Because I puked my guts out
on a complete stranger after
he stuck his tongue
down my throat.

Because I can't
stop
laughing.

I don't want to stop laughing.
Because as soon as I do,
it'll all come rushing back.

All the bad.
All the worries.

Thirty more seconds
and that's exactly
what happens.

The laughter dies
and I wish it hadn't.

Because it felt good to
not be bottled up so tight.

But then we reach El Taquito,
shoes in hand,
and stomachs growling,
and suddenly I feel that same joy
fluttering in my chest again.

Joy like
campechano tacos
and queso fundido
and sipping horchata lattes

on a warm patio
under glowing string lights.

Joy like
Victoria's head on my shoulder,
laughter still rumbling through her body
and shaking us both.

Midnight Snack #2

I know I shouldn't.

On the other side of his door,
he's probably sleeping.

Dreaming in memories
that don't exist
when he's awake.

And maybe it's the alcohol
or the tenderness of the bistec
on a tortilla softer than my pillow
but I know I won't be able to
sleep
without trying.

So I ease the door open,
clutching the carton of tacos
like a sacred offering.

Praying over them
like a priest.

Please. Please.

But as light from the hallway
pools over the bed,
sheets twisted,
blankets on the floor,
I realize that
he's not in it.

And I *know*.
Without searching
the rest of the house.
I feel it in my bones.

He's gone.

Raúl

Lost

Alone
in the dark
I move.

One foot in front of the other.
No direction.
Or destination.

Just going.
Going.
Going
until I'm breathing hard
and my clothes are sticking to me.

Lost on purpose
for once.

And it feels good.

To wander
beneath streetlights
while sounds strike
in the dark.

The bell over the tiendita front door.
Laughter bubbling up behind the gas pumps.
Tires grazing the curb
as music beats
against tinted
windows.

The wind rustling invisible leaves.
My boots crunching through grass.

Sounds that used to be trapped
behind glass,
on the other side of my bedroom window.

A portal to another world
where freedom belonged to
everyone but us.

Is this what freedom feels like?
Being lost
on purpose.
Being able
to put one foot
in front of the other
in any direction you want.

Yeah, I think, *this is freedom.*

Until I feel a tug.

Like there's a fishhook
buried deep in my chest.
Like the tide is trying
to turn me back.

My mother on the shoreline,
reeling me in.

Because when you're made
from someone else's flesh
there is no getting lost.

But maybe there's
a kind of freedom
in that too.

Knowing I can
wade out into waters
unknown,

that I can
get swept up,
flung out to sea,
and there will
always
be someone
out there
waiting for me.

Found

When I find Mr. Villarreal
sitting on a park bench,
staring up at the moon,
he isn't wearing any shoes.

We talk for a few minutes,
about *Wheel of Fortune* and
the price of gas, and
the best slice of tres leches cake
he's ever had in a restaurant
near the Rio Grande.

He gives me hints about
where and when he is.

Not here
in the present
but in 1996
recently returned
from a trip to Popayán.

"You know,
I ran out of money
after just
six days
so I found
a finca,
a small farmstead
where you could stay
in exchange
for chores.

"Feeding the chickens.
Milking the cows.

"But I wasn't
the only one

who needed
a free place
to stay.

"The farmhouse was full
so they put me in the barn
and every night
the horses neighed,
kicking at the door
to be let out.

"Like there was somewhere
they needed to be.

"One night
I finally undid
the latch
and then I
followed.

"Through trees and brush
until we reached a pond
lit up by the moon.

"That's when I looked up.

"Just as the sky
was breaking
open.

"A meteor shower
backlit
by
stars so bright
I felt the burning
between my own ribs."

He presses a hand
to his chest;

squeezes his
eyes shut
and remembers.

"I missed her fifteenth birthday."

"I'm sure she'll forgive you," I say,
trying to be as gentle as possible,
to protect this memory like glass.
Because I'm afraid of what will happen
if it starts to crack.

"You don't understand."
Mr. Villarreal kneads his hands.
"I've missed dance recitals
and
school plays
and
Nochebuenas
and
them being home sick with the flu.

"All because
I can't stop
chasing that feeling.

"This appetite
for miracles
I can never
satisfy.

"That has me
starving
for things
I cannot
see."

He sighs
and there's so much
sadness in it.

When the sadness
reaches his eyes,
they sparkle.

He shakes his head,
breathing hard,
and then the tears
finally come.

I feel my eyes burn too
and all I can think
to do is ask,
"Do you like music?"

He looks at me
and smiles.
"I adore it."

And then without my guitar,
without my uncle's certainty,
I sing the song
Danna chose.

"Es Mi Niña Bonita"

In the quiet
my voice shakes
and Mr. Villarreal notices.

But then he starts singing too,
trying to hide my imperfections,
to ease my nerves
like I'm the one who needs
to be rescued.

As we sing together
that's what it feels like.

Like after running away from home,
after trying my best to get lost,
Mr. Villarreal found me,
and with every fragile note
we fling up to the stars,
he's rescuing us both.

Home

I ring the doorbell
and a few seconds later
footsteps rush to the door.

Danna's mother
has the phone to her ear,
dark circles under her eyes.

Danna's father is crying
as he reaches for
Mr. Villarreal's hand.

Danna is shaking,
looking from me to
her grandfather.

Scared.
Confused.

"What happened?"
"Where were you?"
"Where did you find him?"
"Where have you been?"
"Are you all right?"

I answer what I can,
feeling the shock
all over again.

Finding him in the dark.
Traveling back in time.

"He's okay," I say.
"I think…"

"Whose are those?"
Danna's mother points
at the shoes on his feet.

"Mine."
I wriggle
my toes
in my socks.

She leads him inside
while Danna's father hugs me
and pats me on the back.

"Thank you, Raúl.
Thank you for
bringing him home."

DNA

Danna's father goes
to retrieve my shoes,
leaving us alone
on the porch.

Moths swirl above our heads,
feasting on the light,
the silence between us
so thick
I can hear
their tiny wings
flapping.

Danna steps outside,
closing the door behind her.
"Bad luck."

"What?" I ask.

"If one of them gets inside."

"Oh," I say, remembering
the old wives' tale, "Right."

Danna pinches the
bridge of her nose.
"How did—?"

"I was out for a walk."

"At midnight..."
Her jaw is tense,
suspicious,
and I realize
that she's angry.

"I needed to clear my head.
Things are sort of shit
between me and my mom.
She grounded me.
Took my phone."

Danna meets my eyes
and they're red
like she's trying
not to cry.
"That's why...?"
She exhales.
"That's why
you haven't
texted me back?"

I close the space between us.
"I wanted to.
As soon as I dropped you off.
In the shower.
Lying awake in bed that night."
I graze her hand.
"I thought about you, Danna.
I didn't stop."

Suddenly her mouth is on mine,
her chest against me,
her hands gripping
the back of my neck.

I hold onto her too,
my fingers tangling in her hair,
our foreheads pressed together.

And it feels like traveling through time again
to the rainbow picnic tables at Mena's, the two of us
leaning over bowls of strawberry guava ice cream,
to the day I first saw her, her cheeks burning pink
the second I shook her hand.

And I realize why Mr. Villarreal's diagnosis
is so unbearably cruel.

Because there are moments in life;
rare
perfect
moments
that don't just burrow
deep
in
our
memories.

They attach themselves to our DNA.

I feel it happen.

Another fishhook
sharp between my ribs;
slicing through muscle,
through bone.

And I realize
the only way to cut it out
is to take a piece of me
along with it.

Lucky

The porch light flickers
and I almost think
I imagined it.

But then Danna pulls away,
blushing, and
rolling her eyes.

The light flicks off again.
Then on.

"That's his signal," she says,
hesitating.

Playing with my hands
while I shift from foot
to foot, taking her in
like she is quenching
a thirst I didn't even know
I had.

"How long are you grounded for?"
she asks.

I shrug.
"Not sure yet.
It's been a while since
I've gotten in trouble with my mom.
I sort of forgot the rules."

She smiles.
"Well, I'm sort of an expert.
She'll cool off in a couple of weeks.
In the meantime
do something nice for her.
Hugs, compliments—that sort of thing."

"That's the secret?"

She winks. "That's the secret."

But there's more.
I see it all in her eyes.
A mischievous spark
that makes my knees weak.
And then beneath
her expression,
a dread
because this moment
is as temporary
as all the others.

Because tonight
her grandfather got lucky.

Because tonight
I brought him home.

But tomorrow?

I lean in again.
So does she.

"I'm sorry," I whisper.

She rests her head on my chest.
"Me too."

Bad Dream

The water is running again.

At 2:00 AM.

Who takes a shower at 2:00 AM?

Then I hear it.

My mother's version of a scream.

Still keeping her feelings in a foxhole.

Still afraid to make a sound.

"Mom...?" My voice cracks.

I take a step closer
and feel the water beneath my shoes.

I turn on the hall light
and see it pouring from beneath the seam.

"Mom!"

I open the door,
trying to keep my eyes down.

Her back is to me,
water dripping from her legs
that are draped over the tub.

I feel the spray.
It's cold.

"Mom..."

I grab the towel off the hook
and hold it up. Not knowing
what else to say or do.

She steps out of the tub
and lets me wrap her up.

I press my face into her wet hair
so she doesn't see the tears.

She feels them instead,
both of us quaking.

"It's okay, mijito."
Her voice is hoarse.
"It was just a bad dream."
Her lip trembles.
"It was all just a bad dream."

Numb

After we get her into bed
Uncle Mario and I grab every towel
to sop up the mess.

We crawl
on our
hands and knees
and in the quiet
I hear my uncle
sniff.

My heart wrenches
and I clench my jaw,
trying not explode.

But my body is a stick of dynamite
and suddenly I want to drench myself too,
to hide under a cold shower
until I'm numb.

I just want to be *fucking* numb.

But I'm not
and when Uncle Mario
puts a hand on my shoulder
and says, "Let's pray,"
it all pours out of me.

While he whispers to God in my ear.
While he holds me tight.

I cry
and
he prays
for my mother

and
for me.

For healing and safety.

For no more bad dreams.

Ask and You Shall Receive

The other members of the praise band are late again,
the takeout Uncle Mario brought for them from
Tamale House
getting cold in grease-stained bags that Manny
can't stop eyeing
from behind his drum set.

My stomach growls too.

"All right, chavos," Uncle Mario shrugs.
"Have at it."

We stuff our faces as Uncle Mario stands by the dou-
ble doors
watching the parking lot like all he needs to do is pray
hard enough and Betsy and Jorge and Virginia will
suddenly appear.

But *ask and you shall receive*
is the biggest load of bullshit
I have ever heard.

Because it never works.

Like the first time we visited Mom in prison
and when the gas light came on, Uncle Mario
refused to stop
because he was sure
we'd get there
with God's help.
And then we had to push
the truck more than a mile
to the next town.

Because cars don't run on prayers.

Because Faith doesn't work
without common sense.

"Well"—Uncle Mario sinks
into an empty pew—"you two
feel good about your parts
for tomorrow?"

Manny spins his sticks.
"We got this, compa."

Uncle Mario laughs,
turns to me.

"Same three chords
I play every week."

He nods,
still wishing
I loved it
the way he does.

"In that case, Manny,
feel free to take
the rest of that food
home to your 'wuela."

Manny strikes his cymbals.

"And you,"
Uncle Mario turns back to me
before digging something out of his pocket.

It's my phone.

"I have a few things I need to take care of
before we head home. Mind waiting around?
And hey"—Uncle Mario lowers his voice—
"it's our little secret, okay?"

I nod.

And as he walks away,
I still hear his voice
or maybe someone else's
ringing between my ears...

Ask and you shall receive.

Pity

My phone
is in my hand.
I repeat,
my phone
is in my hand.

Wait!
Does this mean
you're not grounded
anymore?

More like
my uncle
took pity
on me.

And I'm
the first
person
you texted?

Of course.
I mean.
Maybe?

Too late.
You've been
exposed.

So...
When can
we hang?

I don't know.
Mom's been
watching me

like a hawk.

Good thing
hawks can't see
at night.

What do you mean?

I mean...

You found
my house in the dark
once.
Maybe
tonight you can
do it again.

Danna

That's Amore

I used to think that the moon
was a giant
buttery
tortilla.

That the Universe and I
shared
a favorite
snack.

And each time a bite went missing,
the glowing crescent shrinking
smaller and smaller,
Grandpa would say,
"Danna's been eating the moon again."

And then he would blame me for
high tides and hurricanes
while I laughed
and tried to convince him
that I wasn't sneaking bites
behind his back.

Then he'd apologize over pizza
and sing "That's Amore"
by Dean Martin
until the entire restaurant
was singing along with him.

Caramelized Onions, Apples, and Goat Cheese
Grilled Peaches and Prosciutto
Arugula and Mushrooms with Sunny-Side Up Eggs

Pizzas that were works of art.

That reminded him of the
farmers he had met in Southern California
and the tiny cafe at the end of Anna Maria Island
and the graffiti artist in St. Paul who gave him
an unsolicited tour of F. Scott Fitzgerald's old
stomping grounds.

People and places
I'm trying to remember
for the both of us.

Because despite what Mami says
about him deteriorating faster
than the doctors thought he would,
I know that he didn't leave by accident.

He was out there,
in the dark,
under
a butter tortilla moon
searching for *something*;
trying to hold onto
those memories too.

Not the World's Best Pizza

There's a sign out front that says,
WORLD'S BEST PIZZA.

I nudge Raúl and say,
"I'll be the judge of that."

The line stretches from the order window
to the end of the parking lot,
people laughing
and talking too loud
because they're drunk
and happy
but most of all
hungry.

I am too,
my stomach growling
so loud that Raúl's
eyes widen
and then we both laugh.

"My grandmother used to say
that eating after midnight
gives you nightmares."

Raúl snorts.
"If it means
I might actually
fall asleep for once,
I'll take it."

We order two giant slices
of pepperoni pizza,
each one almost falling off
the flimsy paper plates
that are no match for the grease

dripping from the layers of
mozzarella and Parmesan cheese.

If Mami were here
she'd hand me a napkin
to sop it all up
and then side-eye me for
eating the crust too.

But she's not here.

And Raúl isn't looking at me
like this is a test of my own self-control.

He's looking at me
like...like...

"I'm sorry,
it's just..."
and then his finger
grazes my bottom lip
and I realize I'm covered
in sauce.

But he lingers,
touching my jawline next
and then my chin.

I shiver
and smile
and then
I say,
"This is definitely not the world's best pizza."

Moon Pie

The moon is a wide-open mouth
at the end of the street,
the sidewalk sloping down
so that the streetlights
ahead are rows and rows
of glittering teeth.

We follow the light
until the trees
peel back,
revealing
swaying grass and
an empty playground.

Then I take Raúl's hand
and head straight for the swings.

But before he sits down
he pulls something
from his jacket pocket,
plastic crinkling,
light glistening in the sheen.

"We forgot dessert."
He smiles,
handing it to me.
"I hope we didn't
spark some kind of
generational curse
by not eating it first."

"You remembered."

I take the Moon Pie
out of the plastic

and hold it up
until the chocolate
is covering the
full moon.

Then I break it in two
and hand one half to Raúl.

"Thank you," I say.

And I realize why the loss of my grandmother,
Grandpa's North Star,
is so unbearably cruel.

Because there are people in our lives;
rare
unexpected
people
who don't just walk
beside us
through life,
they witness
our lives
too.

They hold our memories in their DNA.
So that when one body forgets,
the other is there
to push rewind,
to cue up the highlights reel
on a love story
that made it all
worth it.

I feel it happen.

Another poem
pounding between my ribs;

about a boy
who finds lost things,
who carries Moon Pies
in his pocket,
who is already remembering
the things I am terrified to forget.

Chew

We cheers,
Raúl holding one half
of the Moon Pie
while I hold the other
and then we each take a bite.

Then we chew.

Quietly at first,
staring straight ahead,
until the chewing doesn't stop.

Until I'm choking
and spewing sawdust.

"It's *so* dry!"

"Yeah, it's..." Raúl nods.
"It's...a little dry."

He narrows his eyes,
concentrating,
tongue working
to scrape away
the graham cracker
that is threatening
to kill us both.

"I don't think I can swallow,"
he says, still chewing.

I tear up
laughing so hard
no sound comes out.

He turns to me,
serious. "Do you know
the Heimlich?"

But it just
makes
me
laugh
harder.

I wheeze
and gasp,
cookie spraying
out of my mouth.

Raúl gets up,
waves his hands
frantically.

"Shit, I don't know
the Heimlich." He tries
to keep a straight face
but the cookie
is falling out of his mouth
too. "Danna! I don't know
the Heimlich!"

He heaves me out of the swing.
And I'm screaming
and I'm crying
and I try to tell him
that I'm about to pee my pants.

Instead,
we spit them out
at the same time,
trying to catch our breath.

And Raúl's arms are still wrapped around me.
And my heart is pounding in my chest.
And I try to tell him
that I think I'm falling.

Hard.

Like Glue

It's 4:00 AM
and I can't move

from this spot
in the center
of the roundabout
in the center
of the universe.

We stare at each other
in the dark
until one of us
breaks into a smile.

Like we forgot
for a second
that we weren't
behind screens
behind glass.

But we aren't alone.

A cold breeze blows in,
tangled with the sound of
music.

I don't recognize the melody
but Raúl does,
his fingers lightly pressing
into my forearm
like it's the neck of a guitar.

He plays the notes
on my skin,
and my heart skips
like it's learning

a new way
to beat.

"How does it work?"
I ask, my voice barely
above a whisper.

"It?"

"The music therapy."

I rest my head against his shoulder.
He folds me into the crook of his arm.

"I wish I understood
the science behind it.
All I know is that
our senses
hold our memories
together
like glue
and if you can
ignite one
you might be able to
ignite
the others.

"So you start with something strong.
Like music. But they say scent is even stronger.
And you expose the patient to it
and then you wait to see if they can fill in the rest.

"Songs…they have a better chance of being attached
to positive memories. They're low-risk. Not to mention,
everybody loves music. And it's not just something you can hear."
He traces a finger down my arm, making the hairs stand up.
"It's something you can feel."

Suddenly, his lips
are warm

against my ear
and as he kisses me
I feel my senses grasping
at the moment,
fighting
to hold onto every
texture,
every sound,
every smell.

And I know that a hundred years could pass,
I could be standing half a world away from this very spot,
still not knowing the name of that song that blew in with the
        breeze
but remembering the second I hear it

the boy who gave me goosebumps under a million stars.

H Mart

When Victoria and I were younger we used to
take folklórico lessons next to the H Mart
and if we could get through the entire class
without hiking up our skirts and flashing each
other Mami and Aunt Veronica would let us
buy green tea Kit Kats and mango boba tea
until we were sugar drunk.

But then I turned twelve and I grew out of
my first pair of tights and I started taking
classes twice a week instead of just once.
And I tried to squeeze into the right shape
even though I didn't know what that was.
I just knew that I was wrong.

That Victoria could eat whatever
she wanted. That Mami controlled
everything I put in my mouth.
Sometimes what came out of it
too. When I was stooped over a
toilet because I thought that's
what she wanted me to do.

Her eyes said it. When the skirt
got too big and my grandmother
had to sew another buttonhole.
From the front row at my
last performance, she smiled.
Proud of me. For fitting into
the body she thought I
belonged in.

Afterward she took me
for boba tea and the girl
behind the counter said,
Hey, I haven't seen you in a

while and I blushed because
she didn't know that sugar
had become a currency;

that my thinness
had too. But she
smiled like it was
nothing. She even
remembered our
order.

And as we
sipped on
our tea and
walked the
aisles
searching
for a few
ingredients
Papi
needed
for dinner,
I spotted
the green
tea Kit Kats
and Mami
shook
her
head.

"I'm not buying you another pair of tights."

Mango or Strawberry?

The guy behind the counter doesn't
recognize us. He barely even looks
up from his phone.

"What can I get you?"
He yawns.

I've been here a million times
since Mami stopped bringing me.
With Papi and Grandpa and Aunt Veronica too.
But I always pause before I open my mouth to order.
Like she's looking over my shoulder, waiting to see what I'll do.

Victoria nudges me, knowing
this is where I always get stuck.

"Dirty brown sugar milk tea."

He clicks his screen. "What size?"

"Medium."

I exhale with my whole body
and then I pay,
grateful for the cash
Papi gave me
so Mami won't see
the charge
on my debit card.

Victoria presses a finger to her chin.
"I don't know if I want
the mango
or
the strawberry..."

She turns to me,
grinning,
and I can tell
she's trying to cheer
me up. To pull me out
of this bad memory
we don't share.

She nudges me again,
laughing,
and then at the same
time we say,
"¿Por qué no los dos?"

¿Por Qué No los Dos?

For Victoria and I
the supermercado
is like our candy store.

Amigos
H Mart
H-E-B.

Leave us alone
in one of them
for too long and
we'll be escorted
off the premises
by a grouchy manager
who Victoria will
shamelessly flirt with
until he promises
not to call the police.

Okay, so that
only happened once.
But it was truly epic.

And it all started with our favorite game:
¿Por qué no los dos?

Like the little Dora look-alike
in that Old El Paso commercial
trying to decide between
hard-shell tacos or soft.

¿Por qué no los dos?

We were only five years old
when the commercial first aired
but the meme lives on forever.

The game is all about abundance.

About having your cake
and eating it too.

(The antithesis to
every fiber
of Mami's being,
which makes it
even more
fun)

Can't decide between
the Takis
and
the hot Cheetos?

¿Por qué no los dos?

What about a dilemma between
the chocolate-covered pretzels
or
the yogurt-covered ones?

¿Por qué no los dos?

Pickled chicharrones or hot and spicy?

Brownie Batter Core or Cherry Garcia?

Piña Choco Roles or Pingüinos?

The answer isn't either/or.

The answer
is
everything.

Dígame

We lug our plastic bags to
Peace Point
and sprawl out
under a tall birch tree
before dumping our bounty
between us and running
our hands over the plastic
and foil packages
like they're jewels.

"Bueno..."
Victoria tilts her head back and tosses
a handful of Choco Churro Turtle Chips
into her mouth, and then with it still full
she grumbles,
"Dígame."

I pop an entire Reese's Peanut Butter Cup
in my mouth, playing coy,
even though I'm bursting.

She whacks me.
"So did you make out or what?"

I whack her back.
"Maybe..."
Then I fall over,
screaming into the grass.

"Danna Villarreal!"
Victoria climbs on top of me
and pulls my hands away from my face.
"Puta cochina.
Did that baboso give you a hickey?"

I wrestle her off of me,
wheezing with laughter.

"No. No hickeys."
That's your thing,
I want to say.

"Well"—she lies on her side,
stuffing candy in her mouth—
"how was it?"

I lie on my back next to her
and close my eyes.

And Raúl was right.
I smell the memory first—
the damp grass and the rust
of the roundabout and
the mint gum he'd popped
into his mouth after we almost
choked to death on those Moon Pies.

I smell them too.
The chocolate coating
and marshmallow insides.
Sweet and bitter with
a hint of his earthy cologne from
being stuffed in his jacket pocket.

One detail spurs another
until I'm in his arms again,
feeling the softness
of his lips, his hands
on my body.

And even though the memory is right there,
so close I can practically touch it,
I don't know how to put it into words.

That we kissed.
That it was magic.
That he already knows me so well.

But I try.

For all the times Victoria
shared the juicy details; the mistakes
she'd made so I wouldn't have to.

I try to tell her that she was right.

About Yeong Kim
not being real or true
or worth shedding a single tear over.

I try to tell her...

that I think I'm falling in love.

I try to tell her that I'm fucking terrified.

Straight from the Fruit

Victoria rolls onto her back.
Our heads press together.
"Let's make a list."

"What kind of list?"

"The pros and cons
of falling in love."

"You think that'll make it less scary?"

She sighs. "No.
But it might make us braver."

"Us?" I nudge her.
"Wait...you think you're in love with Javi?"

She rolls onto her stomach,
propping herself up onto her elbows,
her face turning a shade of pink
I've never seen before.
"Okay, don't judge.
But he's...
actually
really
...sweet."

"You don't like sweet."

"I don't like when it's artificial.
None of that high-fructose corn syrup shit.
But give me that pure sugarcane,
that straight-from-the-fruit
kind of sweet,
and I'll eat that shit all day."

The Pros and Cons of Falling in Love

Pros:
You have someone to give you their coat when it's cold out
You have someone's hand to hold during scary movies
You have someone to order your second choice entrée when
    you can't decide
You have a portable human pillow perfect for impromptu
    naps
You have a human time capsule to hold all your scars and
    secrets

Cons:
You have someone who knows the best ways to hurt you

Raúl

Report Card Part 1

English II - 72
Sculpture - 84
Geometry - 70
Spanish II - 82
Chemistry - 64
Computer Science I - 68
World History - 86
Culinary Arts - 93

Report Card Part 2

Being stubborn - 93
Being ungrateful - 86
Being lazy - 84
Being a pain in the ass - 82
Being responsible - 72
Being respectful - 70
Being godly - 68
Being the son she wants me to be - 64

Report Card Part 3

She doesn't ask me what the numbers mean
and I don't tell her
that I already corrected the test in chemistry
and Mr. Rodriguez is going to change the grade
or that Mrs. McBride has been on maternity leave
for two weeks and forgot to enter my extra credit
or that I had to beg Mx. Bayat to let me retake the last
quiz.

I don't tell her
that I tried.

Because the look in her eyes has my jaw clamped shut.

Even when Uncle Mario stops behind my chair and
says,
"Wow, a 93 in culinary arts? Maybe you should be
cooking dinner instead of me."

His laughter doesn't reach her.

"This is unacceptable, Raúl."
She places the report card
faceup. "Do you have anything
to say for yourself?"

You scare me.
I can't sleep.
I can't concentrate in school.
I can't do anything right.
Because I'm scared.

"Did you hear me?"
she snaps.

I nod.
"I'll fix it."

"Good.
Because you stay grounded
until you do."

Healing

Today Mr. Lim wants to sing Dolly Parton
and watching Uncle Mario try
to hit the high note in
"I Will Always Love You"
is the only thing
lifting my mood.

I stare at the floor,
holding the laugh
behind my lips
and almost lose
it when Mr. Lim smiles
and asks him to sing it
again.

Three times.

Uncle Mario sings
one of the most difficult
songs ever performed
three times.

By the last run
Mr. Lim's son
is standing in the doorway,
arms crossed,
shifting from foot to foot.

Watching us
with unease.

As I lock up my guitar case
Mr. Lim hands me a piece of
ginger candy
like always.

"Thank you," I tell him.
"See you next week."

He smiles and winks.

When I reach Uncle Mario
and Mr. Lim's son
their voices are low.

"So you're moving him on Monday?"
Uncle Mario says.

"Where's Mr. Lim going?" I ask.

Mr. Lim's son frowns.
"To a hospice facility."

The word hits me in the gut.
Hospice.
That's where people go
when they're not getting better.
That's where people go
to die.

"We'd love for you to keep
coming to see him." He hands
Uncle Mario a pamphlet
with butterflies on the front.
"Here's
the address."

The ride home
is quiet,
neither of us
reaching for the
radio dial.

Finally, the lump in
my throat turns to

words. "Does that mean
we didn't help him?"

Uncle Mario eases
to the light. Turns
to me. "Healing
doesn't always look
the way we want it to,
Raúl."

Scared

When we pull into the driveway,
Uncle Mario just sits. His sign
that he wants to talk.

I think he's going to lay into me too
but then I remember
that's not his style.

That's why Mom sent me to live with him.
Because his heart isn't a fist.

"What she's going through,
it doesn't have anything to do
with you, Raúl."

Tears sting the back of my throat.
"Then why can't I do anything right?"

"She's still in survival mode.
Still trying to root out her own weakness.
She's seen the world, how ugly it can be,
and she's afraid of sending you out into it."

"Is that why I'm grounded
until the end of time?"

"Something like that."
He sighs. "I'll talk to her.
See if I can get her to ease up.
But in the meantime...
she's still your mother.
We both have to respect that."

I roll my eyes.
"Even when she's wrong?"

He faces me. "Not wrong, Raúl.
Scared."

Chicory

"We're going on a scavenger hunt."
Danna's smile makes my whole body warm.

And in that split second I forget about Mr. Lim.
I forget about Mom.
I forget that I'm breaking the rules again,
while she's at Bible study followed by late night mass
at the Catholic church across the street because
"Uncle Mario is too modern" and doesn't marathon
from the pulpit.

"What are we looking for?" I smile back.

Then Danna pulls something
brown and rough
from her pocket.

It looks like a wrinkled twig.

She holds it up to my nose, letting me smell—
tobacco and coffee and mushrooms?

"What is it?"

She tucks it back in her pocket,
just as tires squeal up the street.

"Chicory."

Tornado

A girl in a bright red tank top
hangs out the window of an orange Jeep Wrangler.
Her mouth falls open when she sees me
and then she squeals. "You're cute!"

I feel the tips of my ears turning red.
This must be Victoria.
Danna warned me she was ... *a lot.*

She also mentioned how hot she was.
More like warned me,
Danna shrinking as she said the words,
like Victoria was a trap
she knew I'd fall right into.

Like I haven't already kissed
the most beautiful girl I've ever seen.

Like I'm not currently holding her hand.

I help Danna into the back seat
and climb in next to her.

Javi introduces himself.
We dap.

There's something about it
that feels like meeting the in-laws
or maybe—the more Victoria eyes me
from the front seat—Danna's bodyguards.

Suddenly, I'm as self-conscious as I was
when I first asked Danna out.

I just want them to like me.

Javi glances back.
"Hey!" he yells and I jump.
Then he raises an eyebrow.
"You like Bad Bunny?"

I exhale.
"You know it."

He hollers
and then cranks
up the sound
before peeling onto
the street, Danna's hair
whipping around us both
until she's a tornado
I want nothing more
than to get caught in.

Dream-Maker

In 1987, Danna's grandfather
took a trip to Madurai, India,

where he ate Thali feasts on giant leaves
and tried fifteen different types of bananas
in a local market where sarongs hung from
the rafters and cradled napping children
while their mothers peeled cabbage from their
hard husks;

where he drank cotton milk with ginger and jaggery
beneath the remnants of an ancient palace
in one of the oldest cities in the world;

where he learned to slow-roast chicory
from a young couple who owned a
Darshini and were happy
to practice their English with him
as they prepared for their first trip
to the United States.

But not before they prepared for him
their signature butter cake
with the same symphony of notes
as the warm chicory he drank
from a metal tea cup
as he answered their questions
about the West
and they told him the dreams
they hoped to plant there.

Danna lays out the article from an old *Gourmet*
magazine.

"The Road to Honey"
by Marcelino Villarreal.

He never forgot about the flavors—
a tartness like dried fruit,
woody chestnut, and
a sweet bitterness like caramel that's
burned at the bottom of the pan.

Magic, he said. *Pure magic.*

He never forgot about the couple either.

Which is why the article was published in 2008.

Because twenty years after Marcelino
stepped foot in that dimly lit Darshini
he was invited to a pop-up dinner downtown
where he was served a butter cake
that tasted just like that cup of chicory.

"Don't you get it?"
Danna turns to Victoria.
"Grandpa was a dream-maker."

Victoria squints at the article, thinking.
"You're right. Everyone he's ever written about
has made it big." Then she shakes her head.
"But that was over a decade ago.
What makes you think they're still here?"

Danna carefully tucks
the article into her bag.
"They don't have to be."

Needle in a Haystack

My mind races.

There must be *hundreds* of Indian restaurants in Austin, Texas.

What if Danna wants to search them all?
What if she never finds what she's looking for?
What if Mr. Villarreal ends up just like Mr. Lim?

Victoria's voice brings me back to the present.
"So where's the list?"

Danna purses her lips.
"What makes you think—?"

Victoria raises an eyebrow.

"Okay, okay!
So I cross-checked
for restaurants that sell
butter cake
and
chicory coffee.
Narrowed things down
quite a bit.

"Raúl and I will take these ten."
I hear the ding
as she shoots Victoria a text.
"Victoria, you and Javi will take the other nine."

Javi's brow furrows.
"You want us to eat at
all of these…"

This time they both glare at him.

"Sorry!" He throws up his hands.
"Anything for your gramps. I got it."

Silently, I make the same promise
even though I know we're looking for
a needle in a haystack
the size of an entire city.

Even though I know
we may never find
what Danna's looking for.

Even though I
know that
healing doesn't
always
look how we
want
it to.

Not It

Butter cake
is deceiving.

It looks like a brick of cornbread
or the last unfrosted tier of a birthday cake.

Unfinished.

Waiting for something to make it special.

Until you take a bite.

Sometimes crumbly.
Sometimes smooth.
With a whisper of vanilla
like the cake itself is a memory
of something pure and hanging
on by a thread.

Delicate.
Balanced.

So good it makes my mouth ache.

But...

"No special ingredient,"
Danna says, shoulders
slumping. "This one's not it."

Then she pushes out of her chair
while I scramble for another bite
before remembering
that we still have eight more to go.

Hope

We eat butter cake shaped like honeycomb and loaves
of bread,
topped with condensed milk and chocolate syrup and
powdered sugar,
alongside chai and coconut milk and kaapi.

Different versions of the same story
without the happy ending
Danna is looking for.

"Victoria says they're oh-for-six."

I reach for her hand.
"If we don't find it tonight
we'll keep looking."

Her face twists
like someone's just struck
her in the chest.
"It just feels like
we're running
out of time."

And I don't know how to stop the clock,
to keep the seconds from ticking forward.

"When Mom was in prison
the clock was my nemesis too.
Always moving too slow,
making two years feel like twenty.

"Maybe that's why it dragged.

"Because while I was begging it to speed up,
somewhere in the world
someone else was begging it to slow down."

"So you're saying it's pointless?" Danna scoffs.

"I'm saying we have right now.
That's it."

Danna looks down
at her list.

"We've got three more restaurants to go."
I lift her chin. "We might still get lucky, Danna."

She nods.
But I can tell she's tired.
Of searching or hoping—I can't
tell which. But I know that feeling too.

So I take her hand,
leading the way;
letting her feel
that in this moment
she doesn't have to hope,
because I'll carry it for the both of us.

Bitter and Sweet

She asks me to pick our next destination
as if the list is a tarot deck
and she can't bear
to pull the next card.

So I do
and we end up
at an Indian bakery,
standing room only,
where a line stretches
out the door.

We wait for twenty minutes
before crossing the threshold.

"Look," Danna breathes,
pointing to a tapestry on the wall.
"It's the Meenakshi Temple."
She squeezes my hand.

Danna orders the butter cake,
and it arrives sealed in a plastic carton.

There's nowhere to sit
and no time to wait
so we race to the curb
and squat, Danna balancing
the carton on her knees.

"Okay," she says. "Are you ready?"

"Should we count down from three?"

She smiles and nods.

One.
Two.
Three.

The scent escapes first
and there it is—bitter and sweet.
Chestnuts on a forest floor.
Tobacco leaves and burnt sugar.

We each pinch off a piece,
eyes locked
as we take
that first bite.

It settles on my tongue
and I almost think I imagined it;
that Mr. Villarreal's article
was too immersive,
the details almost hypnotic.

Like reading it put me in a trance.

Like I'm standing in that Darshini in Madurai.

"Wow," Danna breathes.

The surprise sticks in my throat
where the cake sits,
soft and spongy,
soothing the rough
tracks left behind by
so many tears.

A salve
like the one
I summon
with my guitar

like the prayers
my mother
sends up
from her pew

like all those nights
I silently yelled at God
until I finally fell asleep.

The cake travels down,
the closest thing to a cure
I've ever tasted.

And I can't help but think,
Is this what food is for?

Not just to fuel
but to fix.

Next to me,
Danna begins
to cry again.

"He had a whole life."
She rests her head on my shoulder.
"He had a whole life before I was even born."

"He still does."
I wrap my arms around her,
knowing that she is at the center.
"He still does."

Collar

I don't bother sneaking in.

The house is empty, I think.
Uncle Mario's meeting with a grieving family,
helping them with funeral arrangements.
Mom's still at church.

But when I open the door
she's right behind it,
still in her makeup,
still clutching her rosary
like it's a collar
to put around
my neck.

But she doesn't.

No dragging me inside.
No yelling.

Instead, she turns her back to me
and starts walking.

Cut

She stomps down the hall
to my room
and my insides
lurch.

"No."

I follow her
and it feels like
falling.

Like I am plummeting
toward
something
and all I can do
is brace for the impact.

She takes my guitar
by the throat,
its body knocking
into me on her way
back to the kitchen.

She puts it on the table
like a surgeon
ready to perform
open-heart surgery.

My own heart winces.

She opens drawer after drawer,
searching for something sharp.

When she finds it,
she holds the wire cutters
as if they are ordained.

She opens the
metal mouth
wide around
the first string

and it feels like
a knife against
my own throat.

A gun against my temple.

I wait for her to pull the trigger.

She hesitates
and I think she can't.

That she won't do it.

That it would hurt us both
too much.

But then she slides the wire cutter
away from the string,
making it squeal for
mercy
before she hands them to me
and says,
"Cut."

Danna

Break-in

All the way home Victoria
begged me for a bite.

But I wasn't going to wait another twenty
minutes in line or waste what little was left.

Each crumb a grain of sand inside an hourglass.

Fuel for a time machine headed to 1987 in a country I've
  never seen.

But first is the lock on the door
that I've been told not to touch.

Like I'm a child with a dangerous sweet tooth
and Grandpa is a jar of chocolate chip cookies.

"You ready?" Victoria asks, unbending her hairpin
with her teeth before silently sliding it into the lock.

I nod and she wiggles the metal pin in the dark until we both
  hear a click.

It's warm inside like his
snores are a roaring fire.

And I wonder for a second if he might be
dreaming of India or Aurora or even me.

But the sound of Victoria's jewelry jangling makes him stir,
his eyes suddenly open and bright like he was
  expecting us.

"Mis niñas bonitas," he coos like he used to when our moms would dress us the same. In matching ruffle socks and giant bow headbands in every color of the rainbow.

When we were small and perfect and safe.

When everything was.

Nowhere

It takes some convincing
for Grandpa to eat a slice of cake
at 11:00 PM on a weeknight.

But not much.

I hold it out to him and say,
"Smell it first."

He nods and for the first time
I notice how quiet he is.

Like he's looking at me
through a pool of molasses.
Like that same molasses
is sticking the words
to the back of his throat

so that all I get when the chicory hits
his lungs is a sigh.

"Do you remember?" I ask him.

He takes a bite
and Victoria and I
both hold our breath.

He holds the cake in his mouth and smiles.

He smiles and doesn't speak until . . .

"Mis niñas bonitas."

Mis niñas bonitas

Over and over and over again.

Not a place.

Not a memory.

Not even my name.

The three of us
sitting on the bed,
breathing in the dark,
going nowhere.

Nowhere.

Nowhere.

Silent Alarm

"What are you doing?"
Mami's voice is ice cold
like a blade down my back.

I turn and she's shaking.

"You tripped the alarm, Danna."
She rushes to the bed. "How did
you even get in here?"

Papi appears in the doorway next,
rubbing his eyes. When he sees
the cake,
he shakes his head. But still,
his voice is gentle. "It's late, girls.
What is all this?"

Mami snatches the carton away
and shoves me toward the hall.

"What did I tell you
about keeping this door
locked?"

"We were just trying to help,"
Victoria offers.

"Help?" Mami storms to the kitchen   .
and chucks the butter cake in the trash.
"What would have happened if you'd
forgotten to lock the door on your way out?
Did you even think about that?"
She grabs me by the chin. "Danna, look at me!"

I boil, wanting to cry
and scream. "What are you going to do?"

I spit. "Lock me up too?"

She shoots back. "It's for his own good
and you know it."

"What good?
You're not even trying
to help him get better."

"There's no cure for this, Danna."

"You're wrong."
I kick the trash can,
the lid still open
and exposing the butter cake.
"When it's just right.
When it's just like he remembers . . .
he comes back."

Mami's brow scrunches.
"What are you talking about, Danna?"

"But you don't want him to come back."
I tremble, scared and angry and about to be sick.
"You don't—"

And then the words are cut off
by a sting,
my face burning
while Victoria drags
me across the kitchen.

We both stare at her, slack-jawed,
while Mami stares at her hand, still pink.

Baptism

I don't sleep at Victoria's.

She wraps me up in her favorite cobija—
the one with the giant tiger on the front—
and she puts on reruns of *Spongebob Squarepants*
before making me a mug of Mexican hot chocolate.

The perfect recipe for a broken heart
if broken hearts could actually heal.

But mine is covered in calluses.
In stretch marks and thick scar tissue.
Permanently bruised like a week-old plum.

And I almost let Raúl bite right into it.
Like it wasn't rancid.
Like it wasn't poison.

"Stop thinking about her."
Victoria smooths my hair back
before tickling my scalp.

And I almost do.

I almost give in to my own exhaustion,
reaching for the off switch on my brain
until I hit the replay button instead.

Over and over until the sting becomes a branding iron.

A born-again baptism.
Forged in fire.
Burying the old Danna
and turning her into someone new.

Bad Bitch Kit

"This clown..."
Victoria sighs
before tossing her phone.

Then we hear a knock.

For a second,
my heart flutters,
and I think it might be Raúl.
That somehow he *knows*.
That he's here to rescue me.

But when Victoria
opens the door
it's Javi.

I pop my head up
from behind the couch
and he gives me a wave.

"I heard things
sort of went to shit."

"Shh!" Victoria swats at him.
"My parents are asleep.
Keep your voice down."

"Oh. Sorry."
He whispers
but it's still
obnoxiously loud.

I laugh.

Then he raises
the plastic bag he's holding.

"What's this?"
Victoria asks.

"A Bad Bitch Kit."

She puts her hands
on her hips.
"A what?"

"A Bad Bitch Kit.
It's a list of stuff
my sisters send me
to get when they're having
a shitty day. So they go
from feeling bad
to feeling like a bad *bitch*.
Get it?"

She snatches the bag
and rifles through it.
"Cookie dough ice cream.
A bag of hot Cheetos.
Pink Passion fingernail polish.
A plush sloth
and a bottle of Midol."
She shoves him.
"Javi, this is some
period shit!"

"Oh..."
He looks down,
surprised. "Well,
are either of you
on your period?"

She slams the door closed,
before turning to me,
mouth hanging open.

"It's actually...
kind of sweet,"
I admit.

After three seconds
she opens the door again.

"Hey,"
she says,
gentler this time.
"Come back here."

He takes careful steps,
waiting for her
to strike again.

Instead, she kisses him.
Hard like
they're in a movie
and he's just gotten back
from the war.

While I sneak up
behind them
and swipe
the tub of ice cream.

I Just Wish…

I skip school and Victoria
claims she can't let me
ditch all alone
and Javi decides it's no fun
to play hooky without a car
so he picks us up and drives
us to Whataburger.

We order three
jalapeño cheddar biscuits
three cinnamon rolls
and three chocolate shakes.

Javi marvels
at the way we down
our breakfast before
we even reach Peace Point.

"Do you guys always eat this much?" he asks.

Victoria eyes him. "What do you mean
this much?"

"Yeah," I join in.
"What are you
trying to say?"

"I just meant
it's impressive
like where does it all—?"

Victoria raises a single eyebrow.

Javi takes a big bite of his biscuit.

"Good choice," she tells him

before throwing the door open
and racing toward the best light
for a quick selfie.

"What do you think for lunch, Danna?
Should we take him to Veracruz?
Or maybe Dee Dee's? I've been craving Thai lately.
Oh, wait, what about Halva Bros?"

Javi throws up his hands.
"You're already thinking about lunch?"

Victoria stomps her foot.
"Javi Montoya. If one more bit
of misogynistic bullshit
leaves those soft pillowy
lips of yours, I'm going to bite
them right off!"

"Whoa, whoa, whoa...
misogynistic? I've just never
met girls who—"

She jumps on top of him,
gnashing her teeth,
while he laughs
and squeals
like he's in love.

And I think about Raúl and I
laughing under
that full moon. Kissing
under it too.

Because he doesn't see me
the way *she* does.

I just *wish*

I *knew*

who was *right*.

Come Home

When my phone buzzes
I'm so stuffed
I can barely
pull it out of
my back pocket.

My heart skips
and for a second
I think it might be Raúl
but then I remember that
he's grounded,
that last night
when we were
chasing down
the perfect butter cake
he wasn't supposed
to be out at all.

But he broke the rules
for me.

Like I was worth it
even though I feel
like that crumbled
cake tossed in the
trash.

And I wonder if I should tell him.
Warn him.

Because if my own mother can't love me,
how could he?

"Who is it?"
Victoria asks, nodding
to my phone,
still buzzing in my hand.

I use my palm to shade the screen
and see who's calling.

Papi.

And when I don't answer
he sends me a text.

Danna, come home.

I'm Sorry

I smell his apology first.

Buttery sugary goodness that quickens my steps
until I see a plate full of bright pink polvorones
on the kitchen counter,
Papi behind them,
clutching a wet rag,
the saddest look
of relief on his face.

I wait for his hundred-watt smile,
for a joke,
for him to tell me
to close my eyes.

His lip trembles
and then he reaches for me,
flour still stuck to his apron,
now sticking to my hair.

And it's the best-smelling hug I've ever had.

I try to tell him that between gasps.

He tries to tell me something too.
In his firm grip, arms wide around me.
In the way he gently rocks me
like he's a life raft and I'm lost at sea.

Papi holds me
and whispers in my ear,
"I'm sorry, Danna.
I'm so *so* sorry."

It only makes me cry harder
because what do those words mean
if he still loves her?

What do those words mean
if after everything
I still love her too?

Los Cinco Sentidos

I tell Papi
all about
the five senses.

How they are the glue,
keeping our memories
intact.

And I explain that
Grandpa's memories
are special
because
he lived
each one
twice.

The first time
he walked into that Darshini
in India in 1987
and again when he wrote about it
for *Gourmet* magazine.

And when I stay up late
poring over his journals,
it's like I'm living them too.

I see his life *before*. I see *him*.

And sometimes
when he takes a bite of something
from one of those memories
he's lived twice
he lives it again
right in front of me.

He *sees* himself.

He remembers.

Break Out

Papi glances at the clock
and I know he's thinking
that Mami won't be home
for another couple of hours.

"Do you believe me?"
I ask, my voice urgent.

His mouth twists.
He sighs.
"I don't know
but...
let's see
if he's hungry."

Craig's BBQ

In 1976, Marcelino Villarreal
wrote a profile
of Craig Campbell
for the *Austin American-Statesman*.

It was one of his first big assignments,
to memorialize the pit master
and the little barbecue restaurant
that could
at East Fourth and Alameda
that survived
two fires
and relentless
gentrification
on all sides.

But they couldn't
tear down the mural
of Martin Luther King Jr.
or the crooked Pepsi sign out front
or my favorite part—the words scrawled
beneath the outdoor order window:
YOU DON'T NEED NO TEETH TO EAT MY BEEF

Papi walks in first
to talk to the girls behind the counter
about Grandpa—how different he looks;
how he's not quite himself
but how we're hoping
some mutton ribs and hot sausage
with a side of yams
will change that.

Victoria and I
each take Grandpa
by the arm

and while we wait
for a table,
I watch his eyes
roam the yellow wall
covered in photographs of
musicians and athletes and
the restaurant's unofficial mascot,
the late Stevie Ray Vaughan.

Grandpa points.
"He flew Craig's
barbecue to New York City
when he was working
on an album with
David Bowie."

I glance at Papi
and my eyes say,
It's happening.

Papi's eyes are suddenly glassy
and he clears his throat
to try to compose himself.

At our table,
employees stop to chat
like Grandpa is as famous
as Stevie Ray Vaughan.

He's polite back
but their faces
don't seem to register
and after a few
awkward interactions
he gets fidgety
and anxious.

"Pa," Papi says, gently.
"What's wrong?"

He doesn't answer
and then suddenly
the table is overflowing with food.

"In case what he ordered
doesn't ring a bell," the waitress
offers. "Craig wanted him to
have the whole menu."

Another Gut Punch

We pass plates
and stuff our faces:

Brisket
Ribs
Mutton
Hot Sausage
and Barbecue Chicken

with Mac 'n' Cheese
Baked Beans
Green Beans
Potato Salad
and Yams.

We
stack
it all
between
slices of white bread
and it's like giving
my insides
a hug.

The meat so tender
you can practically swallow
it whole; the dry rub
cooking into a thick crust
that feels like fireworks.

"How is it, Pa?"
Papi asks.

Grandpa pauses
like Papi's voice
is a surprise.

"Is it how you remember it?"
I ask, eyes pleading from across
the table.

He drops his fork
and it
clatters.
He startles
again
at the sound.

"Pa...it's okay."

"Pa?" Grandpa looks from Papi to me and Victoria.
"Where's Aurora?"

Papi's mouth is ajar.
He doesn't know what to say.

"She's not here," Victoria says.

Grandpa looks her up and down.
At her lipstick
and her ear cuffs
and her bright red tank top.

"Dios mío, Raquel.
When your mother sees you..."

Raquel.

He thinks she's Mami.

Victoria shrinks,
biting her lip
while her eyes sting red.

"And who's this?
Another man twice your age?"

He faces Papi and yells,
"What are you doing
with my little girls?"

Another gut punch,
Papi's face and neck
turning beet red.

"Grandpa," I say,
my voice firm.
"Grandpa, it's me, Danna.
I'm Danna.
I'm your granddaughter."

And then the food is on the floor
while Grandpa hurls expletives
like bullets,
in English and in Spanish,
while everyone looks.

While everyone watches.

Watches and doesn't say a word.

Because it's our family that's ripping at the seams;
that's turned into a tornado in two seconds flat.

Not theirs.

Two Beating Hearts

The closed door to their bedroom
practically shakes,
their voices booming
on the other side.

I've never heard Mami so angry
or Papi so upset
or the two of them screaming
so raw
like they're not human
but hearts.

Two beating hearts
tearing themselves open.

"I'm sorry..." I breathe
into the door seam.
"I'm sorry.
I'm sorry.
I'm sorry."

Because I can't lose them too.

Even though we are broken and bruised
and too good at hurting each other.

I *can't* lose them.

Slow Motion

It happens in slow motion.

First comes the quiet and then
Mami's footsteps down the hall.

She pushes my bedroom door open,
her eyes sweeping across
the pages scattered on the floor;
notebooks and newspaper clippings.

Then she scoops them up
in a rush,
not trying
to be careful.

"No."
I reach for them
but she pushes me back. ·

I rescue a leather-bound journal
and she snatches it out of my hand,
pages ripping,
my heart lurching
at the sound.

"Please. Stop."

But she doesn't stop.

She doesn't listen.

She doesn't care.

She takes the only pieces of him I have left
and leaves me in a pile on the floor.

Raúl

La Virgen

La Virgen stares down at us
while light radiates from above her head
and oil runs like strands of silk
building a translucent cage around her.

The lamp used to hang in my abuela's living room
before she died and her six children
divvied up her belongings
like vultures
scavenging for food.

Her jewelry went to Aunt Margot.
Her cookware to Uncle Mike.
Her plants to Aunt Rosita.
Her power tools to Uncle Josef.
Her clothes to Goodwill.

Mom got her old maroon Toyota Avalon
and everything religious went to Uncle Mario.

Mom must have asked him about the lamp
or maybe he put it in her room before
we even brought her home.

For the past three nights
it's been our altar.

The place where we kneel
and run rosary beads between our
fingers,
Mom getting mad when I
forget the order of the miracles

or mumble too quietly
the words to Our Father.

If she thinks my heart's not in it
we'll start back at the beginning
until I'm spitting the words
from my mouth like fire.

Anger bubbling up inside me.

She hates that the most.

When I fidget and groan
and clench the rosary so hard
my hands begin to shake.

We finish the final prayer
before making the sign of the cross
and when I unclench my fist
the shape is pressed into my flesh
like the wax seal on an old letter.

For the first time
I think
about
running away.

About sending this flesh somewhere new.

But then,
instead of sighing
and making me feel small;
instead of making me start all over,
my mother grabs my shaking hand.

And I remember
the fishhook
lodged deep
in my heart.

Kneeling

She doesn't look at me.
"Every night I knelt
by my bed and begged
God to keep you safe.

Not me.
You.

And every day I called
and heard your voice
I had my proof
that He was keeping up
His end of the bargain."

"Bargain?" I whisper,
almost too afraid to ask.

"I lost something in there.
Something
I'll never be
able to get back.
But with what little was left
of me, I promised to serve Him.
To be Faithful
for the first time in
my life.
If He would just
keep you
safe."

Fire rakes down the back of my throat.

I lost something in there.

I lost…

I squeeze my eyes shut
trying not to imagine.

But I feel it
lapping at the edge
of my mind.

Something ugly
and terrible
that has me
tasting bile.

"I survived, Raúl."
She squeezes my hand tighter.
"Because He let me."

I finally turn to look at her.
But instead of looking back,
she lets go of my hand.

"He's all you have, Raúl.
When you're out in the world,
out in those streets.
Remember that."

Dead Stars

On the other side
of my bedroom wall,
she is still
praying.

Still making promises

like it makes a difference.

Like Faith is a straitjacket
I should wear with pride.

All because she has her proof.

Me.

But what about my prayers?

To keep her safe.
To keep her whole.

Her wings
were ripped out
anyway;
clipped
like the strings
on my guitar.

Leaving behind a hollow drum.

A black hole
that eats the light.

Dead stars.

Choking

on darkness.

Mistake

Uncle Mario is sitting at the kitchen table across from
Mom
who is gripping her coffee mug like she wants to
strangle it.

She looks angry.
But mostly, she looks tired.

"Oye, mijo." Uncle Mario pushes out of his chair.
"Let's go for a drive."

Mom doesn't look up as we leave
and I don't look back.

He's all you have, Raúl.
Remember that.

I will, I think.

And I'll never make the mistake of needing you again.

How You Pray

I follow Uncle Mario
out to his truck
and there,
in the front seat,
is my guitar
newly strung.

I run my fingers
along the frets,
igniting
a faint, tinny sound
that makes
my lungs ache.

Then he squeezes my shoulder
and says, "I told her
this is how you pray."

No One Answered

For forty-eight minutes
Mr. Villarreal doesn't speak.

We sing the Drifters
and
the Beach Boys
and
Jenni Rivera
and
Ritchie Valens

and he doesn't even move.

Like he's trapped behind glass,
a million miles away
and we're nothing but ghosts—
silent and invisible and *waiting*.

. . .

Danna waits too,
leaning against the door
leading into the kitchen.

Watching and waiting
for us to find a cure
that doesn't exist.

Not in a song.
Not in the perfect slice of butter cake.

Danna *waits*
and when our eyes
finally meet, just
as my fingers let go
of the strings,

the last note trailing off,
I wish my mother could see us.

How hard we prayed.
Me and my guitar.
Danna and her lists.

How we *prayed*.

How no one answered.

Present

I sit on the porch steps next to Danna.

Uncle Mario is still
inside,
telling Danna's father
about every hospice facility
we've performed at;
where he's read the
Commendation of the Dying
to people on the knife's edge
between this world
and the next.

I squeeze Danna's hand
and she squeezes back,
both of us
listening to their voices
on the other side
of the window.

She's breathing hard,
stuffing it all down,
and I know that feeling.

Like you're about to explode
into a million pieces
and while you fight
to stay intact
there's also a part of you
that just wants it over.

Because the waiting
is the worst part.

Waiting for a pain
you can't believe
people actually survive.

"Grief
is torture,"
I tell her
because it's true.
"But it doesn't
always feel like this,"
I add
because that's
true too.

She leans her head on my shoulder.
"I'm not ready."

"That's what I thought
when they took my mom away."
I wrap my arm around her.
"And it was true.
But...you don't
have to be ready."

"I just have to be strong?"

"You don't have to be that either."

I replay all those hospice visits
with Uncle Mario; the words he offered
so many sons and daughters and spouses
when they didn't know how to face
what was coming.

I squeeze Danna tighter.
"You just have to be...present."

"What does that mean?"

I frown, wishing
I was as good
at this as Uncle Mario.
"Maybe it means

that being with him
is enough.

"Even if you're sad.
Even if it hurts.
Even if you don't know how to make him better.
Just being with him is enough."

Danna looks up at me,
her lips grazing my cheek.
I kiss her back,
my mouth resting
against her temple
while I breathe her in.

"When you found him that night,
did he say anything? Did he recognize you?"

I shake my head.
"He didn't.
Not at first.
He talked about Popayán
and something about
missing your mom's
thirteenth birthday.

"Oh, and some restaurant near the Rio Grande
with the best tres leches cake he's ever had."

Perfect

My uncle blesses me
with a few minutes on my phone after band practice is
over.

I step outside to call Danna
but before I can ask how she is, she asks me where I
am.

"Lifebridge. Near the Amigos on Woodland Ave."

I can hear her smiling through the phone.
"Perfect. We'll be able to stock up on snacks before
we go."

Danna

Tapestry

We make the four-hour drive in three,
Victoria behind the wheel of
Javi's Jeep,
Javi, Raúl, and I scrunched in the back seat,
with Grandpa riding shotgun.

He sleeps most of the way,
waking up only a few times
to glance out the window
and tell "Raquel,"
"Step on it, mija,
we don't want to be late."

A wink from the Universe,
from Grandpa Past, Present, and Future
that this is exactly where we're meant to be.

On one last adventure
over sandstone and mudstone;
through prairies and brush country.

Toward El Río.
Toward home.

That's what Grandpa wrote about
Las Kekas in a feature
for *Food & Wine* magazine.

"Un Secreto Maya"

The title
a line

pulled straight
from their menu
about the fried quesadillas
filled with everything from
squash flowers to chicharrones to huitlacoche,
a fungus that grows on corn,
considered an ancient delicacy.

The flavors and textures
didn't just remind him
of his great-grandmother
Zyanya; of her grinding masa
on her two-hundred-year-old metate
or the barbacoa she used to roast
in a pit three feet deep.

"Three feet deep.
Three feet wide.
Three days long."

It reminded him
of the women
who came before her.

Our ancestors.

How memories are passed
from one consciousness
to the next.

Through war and disease and destruction.

How it is an honor
to be the keeper
of so many stories.

As we drive within miles of the Rio Grande,
I feel it like rays of sun on my skin.
A warmth from stars I'll never see.

The stories I carry.
The stories I am writing with every step.

Stories Grandpa fought hard to save.
To tell before it was too late.

Like the photos
he showed me of
giant agave leaves—
fins from an ancient
sea creature—
roasting over open flames.

"The flesh popped like pistols
and my brothers and I
would play cowboys and Indians
until the leaves were ready
to be scraped clean
and laid over the lamb."

Stories about food
because food
is the greatest
tapestry of them all.

Between Bites

Tres leches
is perfection
on a plate
on my lips
on my tongue.

The five of us
eat with our eyes
closed

surrounded
by red and yellow walls
covered in crosses and
crucifixes
made from every
wood and metal
you can imagine

and suddenly I know
why Grandpa said
this is the best
tres leches
he has ever eaten.

Because this isn't a restaurant.

It's a church.

Which means
that maybe
God *did*
take me up
on my bargain
after all.

My soul
in exchange

for this moment
when
Grandpa is
weary
but smiling
and telling me
between bites
of the best
tres leches cake
I've ever had,

I'm
so proud
of
you

Miracle

I look up
and then I wish
I hadn't;
that I had kept
looking into his eyes
while they looked back,
aware and awe-filled
like this memory
coming back to life
was some kind of miracle.

Like *I* was some kind of miracle.

But I do look up.

I look up and I see her
and suddenly tears flood my eyes
because the second I see
the disdain
on Mami's face
I realize
that's
what I'm so afraid
of losing.

Not just Grandpa
but how he sees me.

Full of wonder.
Full of possibilities.

A miracle waiting to happen.

Just in Case

Most days
I sit by his bed
and watch him
sleep.

He used to snore
when being in a new
time zone every week
gave him insomnia.

But now his breaths
are quiet and I have
to check to make sure
he's still breathing
at all.

Papi sneaks me
some of Grandpa's
old articles
and I read them
aloud to him
even when his eyes
are closed.

Just in case
the words
are like a
roll of film,
the past playing
behind his eyelids
better than whatever
nightmares have him
moaning in his sleep.

It Turns Out

Raúl teaches me
a few chords
on his guitar.

He sits and sings
for Grandpa long
after his music therapy
has ended

while his uncle
talks to Papi in
the kitchen
about what
to expect.

Because it turns out
dying
and all of the
tiny
terrible
moments
leading up to it
are the same for
almost everyone.

Other times we
sit on the porch steps,
stealing
a few moments
of privacy
since he's still
technically
grounded

(and probably
now forever

since I
kidnapped
him for a
slice of tres
leches cake)

and he makes
me laugh
about stupid
things
that make
me feel
alive.

Callused

Mami still hates me.

But something strange
has happened
and I don't
feel it
like I used to—
barbed wire
in the pit
of my stomach

tears like hot oil
down my throat.

My insides
are as callused
as the tips of
Raúl's fingers
rubbing against
steel and nylon
strings.

I asked him once
if it hurt
and he said,
"It used to
until the skin
hardened
and my hands
got tougher,"

and that's how I feel about Mami.

Her regret is a song I know by heart
and I've had sixteen years
of practice

not being
what she wants.

But the skin has hardened

and I've gotten tougher

and every day
I get closer to
saying goodbye
to Grandpa,
the more ready
I feel
to say goodbye
to other things
too.

Raúl

Lies

He doesn't tell her that I disappeared after band practice

or about my impromptu trip to Laredo

or that I basically assisted in an elderly kidnapping.

He covered for me.

With lies.

About a family in crisis
needing our help.

He *lied* to her.
For me.

And after everything he's
shouted from that pulpit
about
goodness and
purity and
refusing sin

I need to know,
"Why?"

Uncle Mario carries a stack
of warm tortillas
to the kitchen table
and sits.

I sit too,
still waiting
because I don't understand
the difference between
right and wrong
anymore;
what makes a person
good or bad.

Favored by God or cast aside.

I don't understand
this world
where I'm a charity case
to Mr. Rodriguez
and a lazy piece of shit
to Ms. Choi;
where I'm a thug
in my mother's eyes
and in my uncle's
a tool for God's grace.

"Why did you lie for me?"
I ask again.

Uncle Mario looks at me.
"Because somehow
even your mistakes
have brought Him glory.
Because you're a good person, Raúl.
In here…" He points to his chest.
"You are *good*."

Enough

Tonight there is no kneeling.

Instead, Mom sits on the edge of my bed,
facing the window
that is facing the moon.

A spotlight on us both.

And I can tell
by the way
she grips
the sheets,
by the way
she furrows
her brow,
that there's
something
that she needs
to say.

But her lips don't move.

She tightens her grip;
squeezes
her eyes closed.

But the words
still don't come.

I speak first.
"I'm sorry."

She startles
at the sound
of my voice.

"I'm sorry
I keep messing up.

"That
I can't do anything
perfect
or even
right.

"I'm sorry
I'm not
who you wanted
me to be.

"What you asked for.

"Who God promised.

"I'm sorry—"

"No."
She grabs my face
with both hands.
"You are more, Raúl.
You are more than enough.
You are *everything*."

How Small

I fall
into my mother's
arms.

She leans
on me
too.

"I left," she says

and I shake my head.
"They took you."

"No, Raúl."
She grips me harder.
"I followed him
and I left you.
And for that,
I am so
so
sorry."

She buries
her face
in my hair,
breathing slow
until we are both
remembering.

Banana splits in the Dairy Queen parking lot.
Bubble baths and baseball uniforms.
Mom blasting Mariah Carey while she gave me a hair-
cut at the kitchen table.

All the years it was just the two of us.

Back then
I didn't realize
how small
we were.

Back then
it felt good
to be a thing
she could just
scoop into her arms.

The only remedy;
the only safety net
I needed.

Was her.

"I'm sorry,"
she says,
over and over.

Until we are
dancing again.
This time
in D minor.
In the key
of grief.

Mom rocking me
as she breathes
into my ear
"But I'm here now, Raúl.
I'm here.
I'm here.
I'm home."

Holy

Her eyes find the guitar
where it sits
in the corner,
new strings
awash in moonlight,
brass twinkling
like stars.

"Manny drums so loud
I can barely hear you up there,"
she says.

"Not to mention Betsy's
operatics from center stage."

She laughs.
"She'd rather hear
herself than
God."

For the first time
I wonder what He
might sound like.

Is his voice
booming
or soft?

Are his messages
always whispers
or does He ever
shout?

"Would you play something?"

I almost think
I imagined it;
a strangeness to her voice
like an echo.

Like déjà vu.

"Sure."

I reach for the guitar
and clutch the neck,
trying to read her
the way Uncle Mario does,
always picking the perfect song
for patients in need
of a different kind of medicine.

I look at her
and I still feel
that fourteen-year-old
need to *fix*.

To mend her.
Us. Everything.

"Your uncle said
this is how you pray."

At first, I thought
he was making an excuse;
speaking in a language
she'd understand.

But as my fingers graze the strings
and I remember the past month
without it, I know he's right.

That all this time
I've been angry with God
there was no silent treatment.

No giving Him the cold shoulder.

I thought playing anything
other than praise and worship music
was rebelling.

Instead, every night
I was working out a new
melody, I was running
straight into His arms.

How did I not realize
it was Holy?

That when I play
I am Holy too?

So I stop trying for perfect,
to find the *one*
and instead
I begin to strum,
the song I played for Danna
when the screen went black,
the song that's kept me company
every lunch period since I switched schools.

The song that never
seemed finished
until now.

I play for my mother.

I pray for her too.

And for all of the things
that are meant to stay
broken, not because
it's right or good
but because

every sharp edge
makes us who we are.

There's holiness in that too.

Danna

After All

We spent four hours
combing through racks,
me tossing black dresses
over the dressing room door
while Mami growled
for me to come out
and let her see.

Then she tugged
and straightened
and sighed
in annoyance
until we found
a dress that
we both
didn't
hate.

Now I stand
in front of my grandmother's
old vanity mirror,
staring at the seams,
at the lace detailing
on a dress
I will never wear again.

Just like I'll never see him again.
Just like he'll never see me
in that way that made me feel like magic.

Like adventure.

Like hope.

But the longer I look
at my own reflection,
the less I see the
rose-colored blush
and the thick
curled lashes
and the lipstick
in a bright shade
of pink I'd never
actually wear
and the more
I see
the sharp line
of my nose
and the dimple
on my left cheek
and the crinkles
around my eyes
that were just like his.

The longer I look
the more I see Aurora too.
Her suntanned skin,
dark brown freckles
on the bridge of her nose.
Her light brown hair,
auburn streaks
burning bright
in the sun.

In my reflection,
I see them both.

Staring back at me.

Like magic.

And suddenly
it doesn't matter
which pieces of me
are perfect
and
which pieces of me
are wrong.

What matters
is being alive
in this body
that carries
so much more
than just
my fears
and doubts
and dreams.

It carries
them too.

Which is proof
that this body
that I've been
warring with
for so long
is made of
magic
after all.

Moving Train

We bury him at sunset
so Mami doesn't have to spend all day
dealing with relatives who are upset
that we didn't feed them.

She barely even hugs them,
unloading them onto
Aunt Veronica who is happy
to be in the spotlight for once.

I stand at the edge of the tent
and wait for Victoria while I push back
the cuticles on my fingers
so hard they start to turn red.

But she's late
and the mariachi music
is about to start,
which means I only have
a few more seconds
before I explode.

Please. Hurry.

"Danna?"
Raúl finds me first
and I don't know why
I didn't think he'd come
but of course he would
and now he's here and
it's like I've been running
a marathon
for the past several months
and I'm finally at the finish line
and all my body wants to do is collapse.

So I do.

I fall into him
and I scream,
"It's not real.
It's not real.
It's not real."

Even though it is
and it's happening
and this grief
is like a moving train.

I scream and cry while everyone watches.

But I don't care.

Because it's either
screaming into the
wind rippling off
this giant steel machine
or it's getting caught
under the wheels,
crushed into a million
pieces.

Starting Now

"Danna."

I peel myself
from Raúl,
try to catch
my breath.

It's Javi.

"What's wrong?"
Raúl asks,
trying to read him
even though
I already know.

"Where is she?"

I find Victoria
in the front seat
of Javi's Jeep,
her makeup
running
down her face
while she bites
her lip
so hard
I think it might
bleed.

Because for once
she is not in control.

And
for once
I know exactly
how she feels.

"Hey," I whisper
before sliding in
next to her.

We sit,
side by side,
sniffling and shaking,
tears rolling
down our faces.

Crying in silence
until the pain
reaches its peak.

Victoria finally
whispers back,
"Who's going to
argue with me
about the best
weapons to have
during a zombie
apocalypse?"

I laugh
and it's raw.

"Who's going to tell us
funny stories that
make us
spew orange juice
out of our noses?"
I add.

She laughs too,
just as pained.

Because what
we're really asking
is...

Who's going
to make us
fall in love
with the
world?

Who's going
to tell us
we're brave
enough to
make our
way in it?

Victoria sniffs.
"But most importantly,
who's going to
make sure we order
dessert first?"

I take her face
in my hands.
"Us, Victoria.
You and me."

She grabs
my face too.
"You and me."
Then she grins,
the sparkle
in her eye
returning
as she says,
"Starting now?"

I glance at the
reflection
of the service
in the side mirror.

Raúl's uncle leading
everyone in prayer.

Mami's face
hard
and hidden
behind her
dark sunglasses.

Not the send-off
he deserves.

Not the send-off
we deserve either.

I turn back to her.
I nod.

"Starting now."

S'more

The four of us
pile into Javi's Jeep,
skirting
on the dirt path
before heading west,
toward the last beats of light.

"So…where are we going?"
Raúl asks.

I hold up my phone
so Javi can follow the GPS.

When we reach the ice cream truck
there's no line and Victoria
and I hop out before
we're even parked.

"Slow down," Raúl calls.

But I don't want things to slow down.
I want them to speed up,
to speed past this moment
when Grandpa's body
is being lowered into the ground;
past this day that I wish had never happened;
that I wish wasn't here.

I want it to be tomorrow,
Raúl and I on another date,
stuffing our faces with
Thai-style ice cream while
the sun sets behind a mess
of trees and traffic.

I want it to be
a week,

a month,
a year
from now
when
that first bite of
sweet cream
with Teddy Grahams,
chocolate syrup, and
the most perfectly
roasted marshmallow
doesn't make me
clench and cry
but instead it makes me smile . . .

Because it reminds me of what he used to say
about always eating his dessert first.
"You never know what could happen, mija."

But today is not that day.
Today, I don't smile.
Today, I lean against
Victoria, and eat
my ice cream
between sobs while Raúl
rubs my back.

While they bear it with me—
the emptiness
and feeling
of the terrible unknown.

Silent and sturdy and safe.

And then
the unknown
grows those
familiar fangs
as Victoria says,
"Danna,
I think that's . . ."

I look up
and my shelter
comes crumbling down.

Because she's right.

It's my mother.

High Alert

She comes to stand
right in front of me.
A vortex ready
to swallow me whole.

Raúl squeezes my hand,
hesitating for a moment
before jumping down
from the picnic table.
"I'll give y'all some space?"

Victoria eyes me,
waiting for permission
to leave.

For me to say
that I'm okay without her.

I nod and then
I watch them
walk away,
willing them
not to go too far
in case I need
another escape.

She senses me
on high alert
and I wait for it
to make her angry
like everything
else I do
but the longer
she looks
at me;
at the way

I'm trying so hard
to disappear,
the more she
deflates.

Until she's sitting next to me,
our shoulders touching.

My body
shifts away,
still afraid,
and suddenly
she's crying.

I don't know how long we sit there,
tears streaming down Mami's face
but it's long enough for the sound
to burrow deep in my skin
like the song I heard when
Raúl and I were lying in the
center of the roundabout.

Sound waves stitched
over and over again
across every nerve ending
until the echo sounds
between my own ears.

And then it stops.

Mami goes quiet
and then she reaches for my spoon
and leads a glob of ice cream
to her mouth.

An Island

"I didn't always used to be this angry."

Shadows hide her eyes.

"But for so long it was the only emotion that was safe.
Because I thought I could control it."

She shivers.

"But I can't.
And I hurt you."

She moves closer but she doesn't touch me.

"I don't know if you can ever forgive me.
I probably don't deserve it.
But I have never loved someone as much as I love you,
        Danna."

I can't breathe
because if I do
I'll break.

I'll break into a million pieces all because she said it.

All because I wasn't sure
that she felt anything at all.

"I've never been good at showing it.
Not to you or your father or to anyone.
Not since..."

She goes quiet again
but this time it feels different.

Deeper.

Like we've waded out
into the middle of the ocean.

An island
of just us two.

"I was just a little younger
than you are now. It was my . . .
my fifteenth birthday.
Your grandfather was away
somewhere. Your grandmother
was busy wrangling your
aunts and uncles. I was always
such an afterthought to them both.
Or at least that's what I thought.
But she noticed me that night,
on my way out the door, long enough
to say that I was wearing too much makeup,
that my dress was too short.

"I knew it. I looked like a stranger
even to myself. But boys, men too,
had been looking at me like I was
grown for years. I started to think
they were right."

She reaches for my hand.

"Your aunt Veronica bought me that dress.
She made the alterations too."
Her hand trembles and I hold her tighter.
"When she found me I kept telling her
I was sorry for ruining it."
She wipes her eyes and I feel mine burn too.
"He said it's what my body was made for;
what it wanted. Like it didn't matter what
was coming out of my mouth. My body
was saying something else.

"And he wasn't
the last."

I see her,
in her birthday dress,
still just a girl
even if the world
didn't see her like one.

And then I see the moment
that all changes.

The eyes she painted
over and over and over again.

And suddenly,
my mother, hard as stone,
is made of glass,
full of cracks
that I want to gently
run my fingers over,
that I want to hold
the way she used to
hold me when I was
still small enough for
her to keep safe.

"Mami, I'm so—"

She shakes her head
like that isn't why she's here.

"Danna, I was wrong."
She finally faces me.
"For making you think
it was you. Who you are;
the way you look. I was
wrong."

Raúl

The Girl with the Cookies

It sounds like she's wrangling
a bunch of rattlesnakes
on the kitchen stove,
grease hissing
and then striking
with a snap
as something doughy
turns golden brown
at the bottom of her
cast iron pot.

It used to be the only pot she ever used—
for simmering caldo and frying taquitos and slow-
roasting meat.

I haven't seen it in two years,
haven't smelled her picadillo in even longer.

"What's all this?"
Uncle Mario asks,
loosening his funeral tie.

She spoons each fried pastry onto a stack of
paper towels.

"Mmm…" Uncle Mario moans.
"Empanadas."

"Empanadas of the Immaculate
Conception,"
Mom corrects him.

I raise an eyebrow.
"That's really what they're called?"

Uncle Mario laughs
as he scavenges the leftover
ingredients on the counter.
"Named after a fierce nun
who escaped imprisonment
in Spain."

"She was supposed to be
Queen Isabella's companion,"
Mom adds.
"But she was too pretty.
Queen Isabella got jealous
and locked her up."

"So they named an empanada after her?" I ask.

"It's not just an empanada."

Mom cracks one open,
revealing the raisins and
olives and slivered almonds
tucked in the ground beef
like tiny jewels. I smell the
cloves and cinnamon and comino,
my mouth watering.

"It's a story.
About Faith.
About leaving behind what you know.

"About strength."

She hands one half to me
and the other half to Uncle Mario.

"Delicioso," Uncle Mario says,
already reaching for another one.

"No toques."
Mom shakes a rag at him.
"These aren't for you."

Uncle Mario frowns.
"Uh, well, who are they for?"

Mom turns her back to us,
dropping more empanadas
into the crackling oil.

"The girl with the cookies."

Mom, Meet Danna

The other band members
are already onstage,
Manny twirling his sticks
and making kissy-faces
at me from behind his drum set.

I stand by the entrance,
fiddling with my tie,
sweating bullets,
while people smile
and shake my hand
like it's *them*
I'm there to greet.

I smile back
and try not to
seem like an asshole
while I scan the
parking lot
for Javi's
Jeep Wrangler.

My ears find them first,
Ozuna blaring from the speakers
while they pull into a spot
at the very back.

Then Danna jumps out
like she's in a slow motion
music video, sunlight
glinting off her glossy
watermelon lips.

She turns to grab something
from the back seat—a picnic basket.

"Did she bring baby Moses?"
Manny pops up behind me.
"Holy shit, is that the sister?"
Manny immediately starts drooling
and I know he's spotted Victoria.

"Her cousin."

He swallows.
"And the vaquero.
He's a cousin too?"

I smirk, shake my head.
"Victoria's boyfriend, Javi."

"Shit."
Manny throws up his hands.

"You're in the Lord's house."
My mother pops up behind us both.
"Speak like it."

"Sorry, Ms. Santos."
He backs away, slowly,
before disappearing
around the corner.

But not before
mouthing the words,
"Good luck."

I pray for it too,
every step Danna takes
making my heart race.

She finally reaches us
and smiles wide.

I straighten,
clear my throat.
"Uh, Mom, meet Danna.
Danna, meet…Mom."

Next Time

"Thank you so much for the empanadas, Ms. Santos.
They were delicious.
My family really appreciated them."

Mom nods, her eyes softening. "I'm very sorry for
your loss."

"And I'm sorry too," Danna says. "For getting Raúl
in so much trouble.
He was just trying to be there for me. But—"

"But next time you'll call before you decide to take an
impromptu road trip."

Danna smiles, sighs. "Yes. Of course."

And I don't ask how she knows
or why I'm not still grounded.

I already know the answers;
can suddenly feel
the tug
between my own ribs.

That I am never lost.

That I am hers.

That no matter
how far
I drift
away
from shore,
she will always be
the tide
calling
me
back.

I May Have a List

We drop the conchas Danna made
on the breakfast bar next to the
fresh fruit and metal trays full of
eggs, bacon, and biscuits so hard
you have to swallow them whole
or risk chipping a tooth.

As soon as people see the
pink and orange swirls
topped with sparkling
sugar, they race out of
their seats.

Uncle Mario has to pinch his lip
and whistle to make sure service
starts on time.

"I can't throw my panties
all the way from the back,"
Danna teases
and I almost choke.

So I lead Danna, Victoria, and Raúl
to some empty seats near the front.

"You take requests?"
Javi asks.

Victoria swats him.
"We're not at the club, pendejo."

While they bicker,
giggling
like they're on a first date,
Danna wags a finger at me

and I lean down
until her mouth is by my ear.

She kisses me on the cheek.
"I liked your mom."

"I think she liked you back."

Her eyes widen,
mischievous.
"So this means we can plan
another road trip?"

I narrow my eyes at her.
"You've already
got another
destination
in mind?"

She quirks her mouth
and then says,
"I may have a list."

Heaven

At first
when Betsy closes her eyes
and lifts her hands
like she is being touched
by something divine,
my own eyes
can't help
but roll in response.

Because she's always late
if she shows up at all.

Because she never cares this much
when people aren't watching.

But then I remember
my hands
on the strings,
the beating of
my own heart
beneath the beat
of Manny's drums.

I remember
that with
or without
an audience;
whether I'm
singing in tune
or screaming
at the top of my lungs;
whether I know
the notes that come next
or I'm just making them up as I go

whether I mean to cry out
to God

or to blame Him
for everything that hurts

when I'm playing
I go somewhere
that feels a lot like
Heaven.

But as I spot
Uncle Mario
getting all misty-eyed
from stage left,

the way Danna
is beaming
at me from
the front row;

my mother's arms raised,
her eyes brimming with tears,

I realize

that

maybe

the music isn't
supposed
to be
just for me

and that going to
Heaven
doesn't mean

a thing
unless
other people
get to go
too.

Danna

Graveyard Picnic

We approach the plot
like two cowboys
walking toward
a gun fight.

"Do you have the pie?"
Victoria asks.

I hold up the bag from
Papi's Pies.
Strawberry Rhubarb
with a side of
chocoflan.
"Got it right here.
You got the other pie?"

Victoria flips open the
cardboard lid
on the Bobo Brazil—
the spicy deep-dish
from Via Doble
(with extra honey).
"Pie secured."

Beneath our feet,
the ground is still
slightly raised,
the flowers from
the funeral still fresh.

Wisteria
and white lilies
and jasmine.

Smells that only
remind me of
ingredients
in recipes
he'll never
eat
again.

"You feel another freak-out
coming on?" Victoria asks,
gently.

I shake my head
and lower down
onto the jorongo
Victoria's laid over the grass.

She sits next to me
and then hands me
a fork.

"Cheers," she says,
raising the plastic utensil.

"Cheers," I say,
my fork
giving her fork
a kiss.

"How long will she be gone?"

Victoria's voice sounds far away
and I take a bite
of strawberry rhubarb
pie to jolt myself
back to the present.

She's talking about Mami
and her therapy retreat.

They specialize in trauma
and anger management.
She left just a few days
after the funeral.

"Four weeks,"
I say.

"Sounds hardcore."

I didn't want her to go,
not when
we were just starting
to tell each other
the truth.

But "I'm doing it for you," she said.
"For us."

And so now it's just me and Papi
and we've been trying to fill the time
with Food Network
and learning to make
our own pasta
and then stuffing our faces
with said pasta.

But the emptiness is so quiet
and sometimes I just want
to stand in the middle of the
kitchen and scream
until the house feels
as alive as I do.

Because that's why it hurts;
why the pain is almost
unbearable. Because
I'm alive

and I feel it
in every crack
and crevice
in a way
I never did before.

In a way
that aches
and burns
and makes it so hard to breathe.

"Hey,"
Victoria stretches
a piece of cheese
and makes
a miniature jump rope.
"Do you remember
when Grandpa
came back from Singapore
and brought us bags of
Kaka?"

"Oh my God!"
I snort.
"Kaka with a *K*."

"Yes! The corn chips!"
Victoria cackles. "I thought your mom
was going to wash both our mouths
out with soap. But we wouldn't
stop."

" 'Victoria, would you like some Kaka?' "

" 'Why, yes, Danna, I would love some Kaka!' "

I clutch my stomach.

Victoria finally catches her breath.

"That's so random," I say.
"What made you
remember that?"

She shrugs,
looks down.
"I've been remembering
a lot of random things lately."
She smiles.
"But it's kind of nice.
You know?
Like I'll be
folding the laundry
or even in the middle
of a conversation
and lightning
will strike
inside my brain—
a memory
lighting him up
for just a second.

"Like, just long enough
to see that he's smiling."

She bites her lip,
hangs her head back.

I crawl over to her,
lean my head on her shoulder.
"I'm scared," I say.
"I'm scared
I'm going to start
forgetting."

"Danna,"
she meets my eyes.
"I won't let you."

Then she raises her pinkie.
"*We* won't let each other forget,
okay?"

I nod,
tears hot
as they slip
down my face.

"Okay,
we won't let each other forget."

We pinkie swear
and then Victoria leans down
and plants a bright red kiss
on Grandpa's tombstone.

Then she plants one on me
while I laugh and rub my eyes.

"Hey"—
she wriggles her eyebrows
still trying
to cheer me up—
"what kind of bees
produce milk?"

And then we both
yell
at the same time
"Boo-bees!"

Roundabout

He's sitting on the edge
of the roundabout,
using his cell phone as a
flashlight to guide me
to him.

"I take it you're no longer grounded?"

He smiles. "For now."
The smile slips.
"How's your mom?"

I stare at the trees,
shivering,
shrinking,
swelling
in the dark
like one giant lung.

"We've been talking
on the phone a lot
while she's away.
She's trying.
I am too."

Behind Raúl I finally see
the bags of takeout
and the lantern waiting
to be lit; his guitar case
lying open next to it.

"What is all this?"

"Donuts from Lola's,
taquitos from Discada,

Kimchi Fries from Paik's,
and two Mexican Cokes."

I open the box of donuts first,
globs of neon pink topped with
sprinkles and maraschino cherries
and candied orange slices.

"How did you know these are my favorites?"

"Victoria may have given me a list."

I waffle between taking a bite
of a strawberry sopapilla donut
and giving him the biggest kiss.

I opt for the kiss,
climbing on top of him
while he laughs and
pretends to beg for mercy.

When he finally stops
squirming,
our lips still locked,
we lean into each other
and just breathe.

Another island
where nothing
and no one
can reach us.

"Thank you," I tell him,
"for being here."

He sits up,
looks me in
my eyes.

"Always."
He stares
at the food.
"I know it's not the same without him,
without his stories and his memories
but
maybe we can make new ones."

I think about the boxes of journals and articles
that Mami put back in my room; the growing
lists on my bedroom walls of
every dish, every chef, every place
he believed was worthy
of being memorialized.

Not just words
but breadcrumbs.

Because Aurora may have been his North Star
but Grandpa is mine
and even though he's gone
that doesn't mean he's not still here.

In the creases of an old
newspaper article,
in the first bite
of the perfect piece
of pecan pie,
in the bottom of
a bowl of
alphabet soup.

In everything bold and bitter.

In everything salty and sweet and made from scratch.

In every memory.

In every sorpresa.

He's there.

"I'd like that," I say
and then, "I think
he would too."

Raúl smiles so wide
I see those crooked bottom teeth
like Papi's and for the first time
I don't fear not measuring up.

Because he brought me tacos.
Because he already speaks my love language.
Because I don't want any more memories
ruined by a voice that isn't mine.

I want this.

This feeling of being alive
in a body that I love
and that loves me back.

This boy who makes the unknown
feel like the cherry on top of the sundae.

Like the *sweetest* bite
of life
Grandpa
believed it
to be.

Acknowledgments

Writing this book felt like one long exhale. In the midst of the most difficult year of my entire teaching career, pandemic lockdowns, and funeral after funeral, I clung to it in the cracks of my day. Escaping into Danna and Raúl's story every time the real world got too loud. Which is why, first and foremost, I want to thank the work for holding me in this fragile season of life. For giving me a place to mend.

As always, I want to thank my incredible agent, Andrea Morrison, for her passion, enthusiasm, and allyship. I want to thank my editor, Sam Gentry, for the freedom and support to bring yet another piece of my heart and soul into the world. I also want to thank designer Karina Granda and illustrator Soni López-Chávez for this stunning cover art, as well as Esther Reisberg, Daniel Lupo, Patricia Alvarado, Bill Grace, Andie Divelbiss, Savannah Kennelly, Sydney Tillman, Victoria Stapleton, Christie Michel, Amber Mercado, and the entire LBYR team, most of whom have been contributing to the success of my novels since my debut.

Thank you to my family and friends turned cheerleaders who have put so much of their own time and energy into sharing my work.

Thank you to the educators like Mr. Rodriguez, who make space for their students' pain; who give them stories like these when they need them the most. Our young people have spent years experiencing trauma after trauma, from the pandemic to school shootings to racial injustice and attacks on their attempts at simply being themselves. Thank you to the people who listen. Thank you to the people who act. By putting a book in a student's hand or attending a march or donating to organizations that uplift students' voices. Thank you for not standing idly by. Thank you for being as brave as we force our young people to be every day.